TAMBERLIN's ACCOUNT

JAIME MUNT

ENTRIES

PROPERTY OF

You, now.

Let me apologize in advance. You're probably going to read a lot of swearing and other bad stuff. If you can't watch R-Rated movies, you might want to put this back where you found it.

Sep 16 6:40pm

The last living person I knew of was eaten.

I heard a commotion. Most the time things are so quiet that–though some five-hundred feet or so away—it was like a fire alarm going off next to me. Her body banging side to side between the frame and the aluminum screen door, like a squeaky toy being thrashed by a stressed border collie.

She fought hard, but was doomed by the first scratch.

They were doing a lot more than scratching… Between when she died and when she turned, was seamless. She never stopped moving… they only lost interest in her. Most of them. Some remained interested in the almost fleshless being, stubbornly holding fast like lampreys. She went out into the yard and stood there, staring across the road, some remnant of her true being (I think) knew I was here and was not yet sure why that mattered. I hope she forgets soon.

I witnessed it from here, across the road… something went wrong. Maybe with a plan. Maybe in innocently following a routine… Like any of us knows what right or wrong means in this situation…We're all guessing.

I guess, no matter what you think you know, no matter how prepared you are, there are eventualities.

There was nothing I could do for her. Nothing anyone could have done for her except to put an end to the suffering… since I couldn't tell when she died, I can't say how long it lasted.

Surviving beyond one bite was too long. If I had a gun, I would have risked a shot to do that much. I think.

Would I dare? She was already lost. Could I spare the bullet? Of course… If I only had one bullet I would have tried. Could I have risked drawing their attention to me?

I'm having a hard time breathing.

I think… I know I'm next. I feel like my number is up.

I don't know why I even care, but I do. Maybe I care because the thought of being eaten alive by a bunch of rotting reanimated corpses doesn't sound like a lot of fun, for some reason. I don't want to end up like her. I've heard hundreds of variations of that scream—unique, I think, to people who are more frightened than they have ever been, while being in the most pain they have ever known.

My gut tells me I don't have a lot of time. There's something foreboding in the air, a bitter taste in my mouth, as I sit here trying to get the image of her death out of my head. The air feels heavy, like a storm front—I sense the world rising up against me.

She's gone.

It doesn't seem right that mourning her should be left to me. I am a stranger, to her. I didn't even know her name. And the strongest impression she's left me is the image of them ripping her to pieces.

I suppose that's why I've decided to start writing in this. Otherwise, why today? Why at all? How I've been feeling about her death has to be the reason.

There's no burial, no headstone to tell anyone who we are. Who we were. No obits. Maybe if someone bothers, they will find a driver's license on a body. But is it even theirs? Is the face too decomposed to tell? Will the I.D. get thrown aside because the person is just looking for a lighter or a weapon?

Probably.

Do I care who that zombie is? Or that one? Or that? Do I think about who they are? Maybe I should. I care who *she* was. I care that she probably spent all this time thinking about the people she loved that died or wondering if people she loved are dead. She remembered good and bad things about those people. She remembered insignificant things about them. Now everything about them too is gone. She is gone. It's like they never were.

I've spent a lot of time wondering what was going on in that house. In some ways it was entertainment for me, wondering who she was. How did she end up there? Was that her home? Should I try and contact her…

Did she get to die at her home?? Millions and millions didn't. I don't know if you know that or not. I think it's horrible.

I always thought it was a tragedy when elderly people died in nursing homes—I know that sometimes nursing homes are the best and only place for some people. Nothing can be done

about accidents—but when a person just runs out of hours…
when they die of old age, I feel like that should happen in a
place you feel connected to. *Home*. I knew a lot of old folks
who begged their kids not to let them die in a "home".
Wherever that want comes from is strong in my gut. It's a
wrenching, gnawing need—that I know will never find peace. I
am not at home. I doubt I ever will see it again.

I always thought it was one of the greatest tragedies when
people died and had no family or friends. Everything about
them was lost. Can you imagine dying and no one caring? The
hospital having no one to notify? What happens to bodies that
are never claimed? Sadly, I think a lot of people die that way…
since the beginning of mankind.

Lost wallets have people jumping all over them to say, "That's
mine. I need it."

Not people.

I've read about people who've died and are found after weeks
or months, by a neighbor or mailman or something. That
should never happen, but is the death most have faced in the
last few months. And for those of us, if any of us, are left…
Jesus, it makes my heart sick when I think about this too much.
I don't like the idea of people dropping off the face of the
earth. I think it's shitty when people throw each other away.

It's bad enough when someone throws themself away.

I feel responsible to remember her. If someone finds this,
maybe they will remember me a little while.

7:01pm

I keep thinking of this t-shirt I always wore that said, "The hardest thing about a zombie apocalypse will be pretending I'm not excited."

I think about it all the time. Because I used to feel like that all the time. I really did.

I wasn't particular about how the world would change, but it had to be something huge, because I hated the way things were... especially with my life. Now it makes me sick how bad I wanted it, for obvious reasons. There is nothing like this guilt—and, in this life, I thought I'd already known the worst kind of guilt...

But regarding this—I was wishing for death and loneliness, basically. I fantasized about this. What was that about being careful what you wish for??—no—I thought I NEEDED this.

I didn't see the whole picture. I wasn't thinking broadly, back then.

Maybe I keep the shirt to remind myself how I felt and how sincerely and foolishly yearned for catastrophe. All those people I saw die, how many more are dead? Millions... billions... I wished for this. Maybe I wear the shirt like wearing a scarlet letter. Maybe I still wear it, because I'm in no position to be throwing things away. I suppose no one is.

I take that back. I'm sure there's somebody. There's always someone who has more. There are always people who waste without thinking about anyone who has less.

That is *if* there is anyone else.

I'm sure there's somebody.

Who am *I* to be the last?

I'm not strong. I'm not skilled. I'm not brave.

So if I survived there *have* to be others. Doesn't there?

At first it helped to think about all the people who were probably dead that the world was better off without—call me optimistic.

But all dead bad people are more dead, which means more dead….. And I can't think about that without thinking about all the people I can't imagine the world without.

Sep 17 3:21pm

Am I supposed to say "Dear Diary" or something? Bear with me okay. I've never kept a journal before. What do I say? What matters?

Most the time I guess I don't feel like my thoughts really matter. It almost seems vain. I always hated to write non-fiction in school because I thought, *Who gives a fuck what I did on my summer vacation? Who am I to think that anyone would want to know?*

Everyone has a story, so no one's is special or everyone's is, so why draw attention to your own. Who am I to decide something in my life has value to anyone else? There's no good or bad that's happened in my life that isn't mimicked in someone else's. The things that matter most are personal, aren't they? Why would I want to tell strangers about it?

So maybe we should start impersonal. Small talk?

What do you think is going on? What are your theories?

Here's one idea. Maybe this is some kind of parasite.

Okay, here's how I figure: it thrives in a corpse—the eggs and larva are maybe in the stomach and drones or something are in the brain???

And they stimulate the dead to want to eat the meat that feeds the parasites, that creates a new host, that breeds more parasites—that killed the rat, that lived in the house that Jack built.

-or-

People don't want to eat people, but the world is overpopulated and there are a lot of hungry people in it. So maybe some demented scientist created something that gives people a taste for human flesh to resolve the problem. No—a need for human flesh…

Maybe there was an accident in the lab that ended up combining it with the experiments with resurrection…

Soylent Green anyone?

It doesn't matter why.

I don't mean that.
I think it matters a lot.

But there's nothing I can do about it. It is what it is.

And it's winning.

We're humans for Christ's sake—we can destroy anything!
We should be able to beat this.

Maybe we will. ☺

There were some physicists or biologists or something way back when who claimed they'd proven this "could never happen". *Welllll*... it's happening. It wouldn't be the first time science said, "No way!" and Nature said, "Uh huh!"

What's *really* happening?

It's the one possibility I'm thinking those scientists never considered—they don't know everything. In all seriousness, if something is happening that is impossible, then there must be a force at work that is more powerful than fact... or one which *creates* fact. It's the "God Factor":

God can do whatever He wants.

Sep 18 7:38am

The living room is a lot dustier than when I first came here, but that's about the most that's changed. Okay. I had to do a few alterations to make it safer, but it's basically the same room it was when the people that lived here before still lived.

The couch is a dark-brown micro-suede sectional. The ottoman is almost as big as my old bed. There are paintings on the walls—the woodsy scenes that I think must come with homes in this region.

I fucking hate paintings of deer, lake scenes and water fowl. Most of them are done by talented painters, but I just get so sick of seeing them.

Family pictures gather on the wall along the stairs. They are mostly those picture frames that have a slot for every grade a child is in. None of the rooms here look like children's rooms. All of the frames are filled through the senior year. Mine wouldn't have been.

There is one portrait of the owners of this house. I saw the man the day I ran into the yard. I'll always remember what he looks like, even the threads of his polo shirt glare out of my memory. The wrinkles on his hands. The bronze sheen of the house keys.

I have no idea what became of the woman. Maybe she was long gone by then.

-

I read most the time. Quiet activities are good. Quiet activities don't draw any attention. But reading doesn't find me food or other important supplies. Reading's not going to keep me alive.

Maybe it will. If you read the kind of books I read.

Which has got me thinking… How long does it take for a brain to rot?

If those of us who are left can hold our own—I think we just have to wait until all their brains rot—that's no different than spiking them, right?

We just can't let their populations grow. If we can get a system of fighting them off, controlling this, then I think we will be okay. To hell with a cure, should that even be possible—We'll just have new rules, when society rebuilds. When someone dies they'll destroy the brain—it'll be as normal as embalming.

Who am I kidding?

What's a bigger joke—that this will ever be fixed?

Or that I keep saying "we."

-

One of the books I have read and re-read literally a hundred times is *The Road* by Cormac McCarthy. I feel a lot better about the situation ~~I'm~~ we're in when I read it. Our situation is a lot better than the man and boy's. The only thing that is better for them is that they aren't alone. Right now I feel that way... Most of the time I'm grateful I don't have to worry about anyone else, much less a child. Much less my own child, if I had any.

The world that was, I often thought, was no place to raise a child. I am grateful now how steadfastly I objected to the idea of being a mother, but am sorry for my friends who are. Have they managed to keep their families together? What would become of their hearts and minds if the answer is "no"?

While I don't have troubles like those, there are some pressing issues that are leaving me sleepless these days—namely the dwindling amount of supplies in the larder. I don't want to end up on *the road*, any road. I don't know what's out there. I only know where I've been before and a lot has changed since I wound up here.

Sep 19 about 8 am

I have no idea what the statistics were before all the statistic keepers died, but when I was little it was something like one in five children will be molested. I had five really close friends, when I was a little kid.

Five out of five of them had been sexually abused—if the same margin of error was applied to every statistic—I dunno. Just thinking—What were the odds before that the dead wouldn't stay dead?

I guess the gist of what I'm saying is, we never had a chance.

P.S. God Bless canned food with tabs.

Sept 20 5:07pm

Romero gets a lot of credit for zombies. I've heard people say he invented the idea of living dead. Never heard of Frankenstein? How about the Bible?

I will say he did make them cool though.

I sometimes wonder what he'd think about all this. Did he believe it was possible? Why? Why did his fiction end up so close to what really happened?

Maybe a lot of people knew this would happen someday—
every one of them praying not in their lifetime.

The Mesopotamians may have been the first. The couple-
thousand-and-then-some-years-old (I used to remember) *Epic
of Gilgamesh* described what happened to the world just a few
months ago. It said:

*"I will knock down the Gates of the Netherworld,
I will smash the door posts, and leave the doors flat down,
 and will let the dead go up to eat the living!
And the dead will outnumber the living!"*

…I think that about sums it up.

Anyone Christian has been drenched in the impermanence of
death. It's all over in the Bible. Death is no done deal.

It isn't.

I've been thinking… When you destroy their brains are you
really just stopping their ability to function? Is whatever made
them reanimate still present, wanting to kill and eat us, but it
just can't do anything anymore?

When I dispatch them now, and they lay there staring, their
clotted blood stuck like jam at the wound, I wonder if they are
truly done. I know if you're not careful with their blood, their
nails or their teeth, that they are just as dangerous in their
second death. It's troublesome to think that there's still
something going on inside them.

What's the worst possible thing that could be going on inside
them?

The person they were. That is the worst thing—that the minds of who they were are always present, and had to live through the first death, existing only for the consumption the living and then a horrible, but impermanent second death—leaving them waiting until decomposition ultimately frees them.

I dreamt of my good friend Marie… she is a mother of two. A wife—a good wife. An honest woman who is trying to do what seems almost impossible: to have a family and marriage that lasts. I once dreamt through her eyes. I dreamt the oozing wound in her arm, scalloped and crinkled like a potato chip. And I dreamt her protesting and horrified screams as the body she once commanded devoured her children.

The worst possible thing is if the person they were, still is.

Sep 27 5:15pm

On a family trip when I was about seven, I had to use the bathroom at a bar full of rowdy looking biker men. I'd never been in a bar before, so I was afraid even before I got inside. I still remember the jukebox, playing something by Neil Diamond or Neil Young. The words are clear in my memory, but are incoherent when I try to conjure them in voice or paper.

The men were loud and scary and seemed huge. I carried a stigma toward them that was entirely unfair. But I was a child and believed almost anything people told me about any type of person. I remember how they looked to me, their style like Paul Bunyan in leather, denim, and angry t-shirts. Lots of skulls and bald eagles. You'd never guess I'm from the Midwest, would you?

Anyway, I thought I would never feel that vulnerable going to the bathroom again. Even though I'm in a house, I just keep thinking, what if something happens right now?

It would figure.

The *whole world* got caught with its pants down.

I'm on the pot right now—I've been backed up, I think. And colicky when I'm successful. My diet isn't the greatest. These days I'm cutting back more than ever. So maybe there's nothing to pass.

I have really tried not to think about this, but food just isn't going to appear in the cupboards. I'm going to have to go out. I've never done a successful supply run. I tried, once. One time had been one time too many. It almost cost me everything— even if "everything" is adding up to less and less. What little "everything" is, however, has even more value. Ahh, the power of supply and demand.

I'm scared to go out there.

I thought I knew what it felt like to be hungry, before. There were plenty of days where I went without meals by my own choice and without. I knew what it felt like to have the acid slushing around, lonely in my gut, possibly looking at the lining of my stomach and considering it.

The longest time I went without was when I left home. I was hoofing it cross country for a new life or *anything* better than I knew in my old one. It was three days before I met the farmer who agreed to put me up in exchange for working at his dairy farm.

I never really believed him when he said he had planned to hire someone anyway, that I might as well have the job. His kids were old enough to help and they often worked right beside me. His wife wasn't lazy. And he already had a few hired hands who *weren't* given a room or meals.

He did a dangerous thing taking me in. I could have been anybody. It kinda made me mad that he would take a chance like that when he had kids in the house, but mostly I was grateful. I have no idea where I'd be if he hadn't come along or if the wrong someone else had.

That's really the situation I'm in again, as far as other people go…if there are other people—what if they are bad? How will I know? What if they are good? If they are good would I be in more danger? They'd be afraid of the same things I am. If they have loved ones, they might not be willing to take the chance that farmer did…

Well, looks like nothing is going to happen.

Am going to check my supplies.

Sep 28 1:21pm

I had raspberries and red clover for lunch.

It took forever to pull all the little pink blossoms out of the clover, but wasting time isn't always a bad thing. It distracted me and my rumbling stomach.

I'm always nervous about eating things from outside—I'd never eat anything I didn't recognize, even if I had one of those field books I wouldn't take any chances—there's no room for taking chances.

One thing that really bothers me is wondering what touched it before I found it. I don't know how this "sickness?" works. If a dead person went by, it wouldn't necessarily damage the plant—it might just drip on it. Brush against it. I can't help but think about that kind of stuff. A person could drive herself mad trying to think of everything she should consider. And she would starve to death... I guarantee it.

Would I rather starve? I don't know what it feels like to come down with this—virus, affliction, illness, plague... whatever you want to call it. I know you're doomed if you're bitten or they get their fluids in you. In some zombie fiction even scratching and clawing will do it. I'm pretty sure that's true.

You only know if you know and then it's too late, for somebody.

All I know is they suffer.
You suffer when you starve.

Call it stubborn or stupid—I'd take death that's not an abomination to reality. But I'd come back anyway, wouldn't I?

I want to clean my food. I can't waste drinkable water to wash food. I don't think I could drink the wash water after—would kinda defeat the purpose.

So what do *you* do?

This is all I can do...

It looked okay.
Down it goes.

No hospitals. No doctors or nurses. No EMTS. Healthcare
workers were the first to go because they were the first to see
it. I read an article about a coroner who was bitten by a recently
"deceased" patient. People thought the biter hadn't really been
dead and had woke up scared and in some kind of panic. I bet
that kind of thing happened a lot. I *know* it did.

The next part happened fast. Chaos. Everywhere.

Somewhere in that *Danse Macabre* were the policemen and
firemen and other emergency people, including the National
Guard and, eventually, all the other soldiers too. My bet is that
there aren't a lot of good people left, even ones that aren't
skilled. If they were good and had skills that permitted them to
help, then they probably didn't survive. And if they were good
people who had the will that demanded that they, at least, try to
help… they are almost definitely gone.

Odds are there are some of them *somewhere*, but I'm feeling a
little bitchy about statistics right now. I go back and forth with
the "I'm sure's" and "I-can't-really-know's."

How about this? I'm sure I'm not the only person left, even if I
don't have any proof. So that hypothetical somebody or bodies
might know how to take care of medical stuff, but it doesn't
really matter because they aren't here and, depending on what
kind of person they are, I might be glad of that.

I don't feel worthy of being the last.

I don't want to be.

Anyway, the point is: I can't really know.

Just like I don't know what to call *them*. Ghouls, zombies, undead, draugr (maybe my favorite), maybe just "dead"? I'll try to think of something unique.

I *am* sure what I am though—I'm living and I have no intention of joining their club.

Sep 28 1:33pm

Do you like this?

"Busy Bodies"

Sep 29 7:28am

While it's amazingly pretty, it's feeling like autumn—a little too sincerely today.

What's pretty? The sunrise and everything it's touching.

Again and as always, I wish I had a gun. There are 13, 14, 16 deer in the field across from me. Their coats are warm, almost red in this light. Too soon they will all be a dull gray-brown. For now, they are lovely. Though I bet they have asshole looks on their faces—every one of them is watching me and knows I can't do a damn thing.

I'm imagining that "hump day!" camel-look on their faces, their mandibles slightly askew, looking vacant. With deer *that* part is kinda a give-in. I would kill for a venison steak. I wish I could kill them for a venison steak... caramelized onions and a baked potato or two... or three.

I'm sure the people who lived around here had guns—this is America for fuck's sake—but I'm not desperate enough, yet, to try and find out.

Maybe that's not planning ahead, but I don't want to get smoked by someone just trying to protect their place and, who knows, what else or *whom* else.

Besides, there has been some extensive looting. I might not even find anything useful. If it was useful it'd be gone, right?

Not necessarily, I guess. Most the looters I saw were grabbing stuff like TV's and computers—when there was no power! They deserved to die just for being so stupid, but the stupid probably got them killed in the end, anyway. I hope so. I fucking hate human vultures.

A long time ago, I had a couple people come by, interested in this place, but I moaned and shuffled and followed them to each entrance they considered breaking in through. I had the place locked up pretty tight and I guess between that and wondering how many zombies they had to deal with, they changed their minds.

If you thought strangers were not to be trusted before—I've watched enough "end of the world" movies to be conditioned to worry that many people can quickly and irrationally degenerate into murderous, raping, feral psychopaths.

Realistically, we're all scared, aren't we?

I just think there are a little too many people out there that were probably thrilled with the collapse of society. Probably a lot of really bad people that were only controlled by "consequence" before—just barely, if at all. There has never been a shortage of murderous, raping, feral psychopaths, has there?

For how much I longed for this, I should have been among those thrilled about it, but I didn't get so much as a moment of ignorant bliss. I didn't want this because I hated the rules. I didn't want this because there were horrible fantasies I longed to play out.

All I wanted was an OUT—out of my life.

I'm not a monster. I'd like to believe I'm not capable of becoming one. Everyone has their breaking point, sure. But not everyone becomes abhorrent.

I haven't killed a living person.
I don't feel great about killing the dead.
What will I do if I meet someone?
What if they were good?
What if they were bad?

How could you know?

You couldn't. So how could you take the chance?

It's better to be alone—no chances—not even with plants—so why would I take a chance with a person?

Even if I didn't see anything, I'd *have to* know they were armed. Who wouldn't be?

Their intentions? Anyone's guess.

I never tried to contact that woman. My actual house, my *home*, is just down the road. Was she my neighbor?

Hell if I know. Never met many neighbors. I didn't trust strangers before.

Strangers with candy.

Damn. <u>Damn.</u>

I'll say I couldn't resist—what? That's the first social warning we learn, right? Beware of strangers. How could they know how powerful the temptation of candy would someday be?

How tempting human companionship would be?

I once ached to have babies.
The need was so strong, I quickly and impatiently researched how to do it without "help," because I was single.

I'd never want to deal with a baby in this situation but I often dream of dealing with a man. It's pretty realistic that I'll die without having been loved by anyone but friends. Not the same thing, is it? There are a lot of things I'll never know. Most of the time it's not a big deal. When you're horny—that's a BIG DEAL.

I'm not, right now.

I'm a couple days from my period and the monthly surge of "Give me a man, *any* man" has subsided and fear is taking its place.

Busy Bodies are so much more aggressive when it's "that time of the month". They can tell. It's been enough months now that I know—no coincidence.

Their eyes only have life when they sense life and they're so fucking creepy—creepier when they know you're there. That ugly, horrible spark... almost like a light comes on inside those bizarre, pale eyes. But you know that. Don't you? Maybe you know exactly what I'm talking about...

You definitely don't need to be told they're creepy.

The deer just took off with a cloud of what looked like a thousand birds—there are ~~zom~~ Busy Bodies in the woods over there. Shit...

There's a red fox crossing the road. It slips like fluid through the tall grass. Soars up the hill with the smooth motion of an oriental dragon. It's going to come right past me—it looks like it's on fire.

It passed within ten feet! That was special. I'm going to hold onto that one. That memory. It looked right at me.

I'm inside now. The dead are coming fast.

They are mobile terror when they wander... they are Hell on Earth when they are urgent. Their eyes are bright, alive and knowing... there is something to feast on...

Most of the time I can smell when they are near. There are plenty of bodies around, but I think moving makes them stink worse. That makes sense since movement might pull the flesh apart, exposing fresh rot and anything festering, to say nothing of them bumping into things or falling.

The sour smell they give off is stronger. Riper.

I checked my list (I made a Zombie Tracking Chart) and most of these are new. I don't like new... I wonder why they are here. I always assume it's because of me. From how far away can they sense me—sense menstruation. I used to be able to wonder if it was the woman across the street causing these influxes of the dead. She wasn't young, but she wasn't that old either... she very well may have still been a bleeder.

Through a window, I look down the tall, untended slope of lawn, past a wrecked vehicle. There are homes on either side of me, but all three houses are on slightly raised lots because a creek separates us. The water divides the properties and cuts through the middle of this property's front lawn. The house, where the woman stayed, is kitty-corner to the left. The field is just beyond that and goes far to the right. All the properties have plenty of yard on the front, back and sides. Most the lots, I'd guess, are three to four acres.

-

Other than thinking that everyone in the neighborhood was lazy about mowing their lawn, a minute ago no one would have ever guessed there was anything wrong here. Nobody's homes are falling apart. The road isn't overgrown or cracking into pieces. This doesn't look like the apocalypse. It just looks like everything is gone... if you ignore the remnants of the woman across the street. The smear across the patio and stairs to the front door, where they got her. If you ignore the wrecked vehicles and the perpetual smell of something burning far away...

If you ignore the remains of all the other people that died, who still lay where it happened to them. Not to mention the half dozen or so dead that are not laying where they died, but are staggering across the "like new" road and up the driveway—other than that—you would never guess anything was wrong here. My lord, there are an awful lot of them…

The fox may have got me—it got the dog barking.

I've battened all the hatches and am now playing the waiting game. Waiting is all I can do.
In a moment or two I will hear them trying all the conventional ways to get inside. If there are too many at those places, or some realize their efforts are fruitless, they start pawing at the walls…

I don't know what's working for other people, but I've moved all the cabinet doors onto window frames so I can close up shop quick and securely—I hope, securely.

Windows that make me particularly vulnerable and/or aren't good "look outs" I've covered with doors, which means there are very few doors left to close between me and them, if they get in.

Adios bathroom door, closet and pantry doors. Exit doors and my bedroom door are most important, and the only still intact. That's the best I can figure to do. Though, I never stop wondering if there's anything more.

I have a dog.

No, I'm not completely alone. That's partially why, right now, I'm not desperate enough to take chances with strangers, but as you know that's not even an issue for me right now. What is an issue right now is "killing" these busy bodies—because they're not going to go away. I don't think they're going to… Not when a meal is calling out—barking out at them.

His bark is high pitched now—breaking like doggie puberty—it's much lower when it's something living. This unimpressive, squeaking bark is like the dog's version of a frantic, hysterical scream, I think.

If you believe that animals have senses that we don't, then what are their senses telling them about what's happened to people. Do they know why this is happening? If they do, is it scarier for them?

What has it meant for them protecting their masters? What goes through their minds when their master becomes undead—a master who would never hurt anyone before? Do they trust their master anyway and stand there for the first wretched bite? Do they know something ungodly has happened, the strange sixth sense some believe animals have—and as such they are filled with a horror and understanding that we humans have never been able to understand?

Some people believe that animals can sense spirits and demons… and they can tell a person's secret nature. Never trust someone your dog doesn't trust. I do think all of that means something, but I don't know what or why. But I do believe they are more sensitive than us—they have keener senses. Maybe if we had the senses of dogs and primitive instincts, we too would be able to smell a wolf in sheep's clothing.

Of one thing I am certain, he gives me comfort...

Dogs are always doing a duty—the best, move toward what they bark at—or they brace their paws and stand their ground—even if they're actually terrified, actually screaming—*if* they're a "good" dog and holds their ground, no matter how scared they are.

Too scared not to be brave.

This thing that kept people from staying dead cost dogs that cower and hide and dogs on chains their lives.

I guess it has probably taken its share of the brave dogs too.

I'd bet it's cost us a lot of heroes.

I know it has.

This dog is a brave bigmouth.

He keeps looking back at me between spells of head-pounding yips. I haven't decided if he does this because he wants me to do something, and keeps looking at me to see when I do it, or if he looks back to see if I approve. If the latter is the case, then my clamping my hand around his mug, tying a sock around it, swatting his furry bum or yelling at him obviously isn't getting the answer across.

His well-meaning bark will be the death of me. If it is, I hope he can take care of himself. He'd been on his own for, at least, a little while before scaring the hell out of me. That's how we met. He tried to give me a heart attack.

Okay—I need to deal with this. These pieces of rotten crap will wander off if you hide well enough, <u>most</u> of the time, but the dog is going off—they'll just stick around. They do not get tired or bored, that I know of… that means they will be here even after they are too rotten to move.

There's nothing predictable about the dead, yet—I am sure I will come to understand how they work and why some behave differently than others, or at least, be able to tell which ones do what. While they, physically, only vary as much as they people they were… they do not all hunt the same.

If you have ever played *The Elder Scrolls: Skyrim* then you know all about draugr. Sometimes the dead behave like draugr (which are undead too), in that some draugr are aggressive and just come after you, like they have a score to settle—while others, you don't even know if they're going to do anything or if they are just dead. You can get close to them and nothing will happen. You begin to think nothing will *ever* happen and suddenly this completely harmless, mummified body comes after you.

In the game, it didn't take long to be able to tell that the ones who were dressed were the ones that would attack. I wish it was that easy to tell!

In the game, I would shoot those from a distance and be done with them. I can't do that. Not only do I not have the means, but I would have to shoot every body laying around—because you just can't tell. It sucks. It sucks to walk by a stinking corpse and suddenly have them lunge at you, snapping with teeth, elongated by gums shrunk back with decay, the neck stretching out—snapping at your leg like a turtle.

Every time is risky.
I hate taking chances.
I'll write again soon?

Sep 30 8:09am

Hi – in case you haven't heard it in a while, how are you?

I wish I knew. I wish I knew there was a you.

Don't need to say, obviously things went well yesterday—dealing with the dead. I'm not going to get sick.

If I get bit, it'll be the first and last thing I write that day.

"One of *them* bit me."

-or maybe just-

"Bitten."

That'll more or less sum up everything, won't it?

I hate cleaning up. I'm really nervous about the right way to dispose of the bodies. Should I try to burn them? What if I breathe the smoke—for all I know that could get me sick. There's no room for fucking up—so far just breathing their rotting flesh doesn't make me sick in any way I wouldn't expect it to. I worried about it that...

I don't like to touch them. That's a *whole* other realm of psychological harm, right there. I have seen parts of people's insides I was never supposed to see. I have pulled arms out of sockets. I have pulled sturdy arms and had the head fall off or the torso rip in two, spreading a track of black and rotting filth like the bottom tearing out of a heavy garbage bag.

Most of the time I drag them by their feet because I don't like the feel of their hands in mine. I tried holding them by their wrists, but sometimes their fucking fingers would brush my arms and it would take days for the sensation to go away.

I'm a little childish with my mess. I just hide it.
Usually around back…
Out of sight, mostly out of mind.

That's cleaning up *them*.

Cleaning myself is another challenge. I got leeches on me the first time I washed up in the creek. Once, on a hot and sunny day, I saw a green striped snake swimming in the creek…only it turned out not to be a snake—but a leech! It was sooo long! It was longer than my hand. I'm five foot-eight, so I don't have tiny hands, but they aren't paws either. It must have been nine inches long. It was so disgusting.

When I realized I didn't have much choice but to use the creek or go dirty, I was once caught off guard by some busy bodies. I am alive only because they do not know how to slink through water.

They must have already been out in the rushes, because I would have heard when they came crashing in. I think they were muddled down in the thick bottoms, deep water and dense reeds. There was roughly ten seconds of splashing before they reached the spot where I had just been… I was clawing my way up the bank and running breakneck for the house. The cattails and reeds are roughly eight feet tall where it's deep enough to bathe.

Okay, I *could* wash up in shallower water—I often do. But if I see someone before they see me, and I'm in deeper water, I can hide in a split second. I've never had to do that, but at least I'd have the option to.

I had a really close call with the busy bodies that day…

I've had a lot of close calls. They have surprised me too many times, but that was before the dog. I don't know what his name *was*, no collar, but now he's Mr. Ages.

When I was little, he was one of my first favorite fictional characters.

I like rats. I have always like rats, mice… rodents. But mostly rats. I have been drawn to them since I was a child. I think I feel kinship to them. I have always thought about how we, humans, are so much like them. Our adaptability. How we thrive. Overpopulate. Make everything filthy and nasty. What we are willing to do to survive—what we have already, can and will survive…

We're probably a lot more like each other than most people would want to admit.

No, it's probably not a good thing for a child to feel kinship to rats, but I did. I sympathized with them and thought they could understand what I was going through. Thinking an animal can understand you is a lot easier than submitting yourself to another person's understanding—who hasn't been burned trying to do that???

I hope you know <u>Mrs. Frisby and the Rats of NIMH</u>. If you ever have to shelter in a library maybe see if they have it. It's

by Robert O' Brian. I don't know that a library could ever feel thoroughly "cleared".
Be careful.

Unless the dead can read, I feel safe assuming you're alive.

Do you ever feel guilty?

I don't know how it is for other people, but even with so few things to enjoy, with the way things are—when I do feel good, I also feel like someone's slapping my hand and saying, "How can you be happy? Better people than you are dead."

And the invisible slap is always there to remind me about foods I will never taste again. *That* person is never going to get to eat anything ever again—be grateful!

They're never going to write a song again.
You're never going to read a book by him again.

Those people you loved—Hell, they're never going to see a sunrise. ANY sunrise, <u>ANYTHING</u> again.

I feel forbidden to enjoy anything too much. Sometimes at all. Regret and sympathy are probably the culprits—but I also want to care that they're gone. Someone needs to care that those people didn't make it, because they deserve to be missed. So sometimes I feel unworthy of still being able to have those things. Any *things.*

I feel a lot of guilt.

Sometimes I think it's all I feel.

So, when I want to feel better, I think—at least, there is no more war and—well that murdering bastard is gone—or that worthless piece of shit is surely gone too—or, I wish I could have seen that person die because I actually truly fucking hated them and they probably deserved worse—I always, always, always end up in the land of:

Damn, I'm never going to hear a new song by this person.

I'm never going to know if this person or that person is alive—
I <u>want</u> them to be alive.
Are they?
Have they suffered?
Are they dead?
Some of the shows I watched religiously; books I always read—

Quoth the Raven, "Nevermore."

Anyway… more blah, blah?

I'm one of those people who get desperately involved in the well-being of fictional characters. I'm no stranger to sobbing for and my heart, in earnest, hurting for people and creatures that never were. Is that foolish?

When I was pretty little I, like most children, read or was read, the Winnie-the-Pooh books. I remember being stricken with a sense of loss and sadness and really, really felt that my stuffed animals had feelings and perhaps even lives.

The first book I recall making me bawl was the same book where my love of dystopian fiction was born—in third grade when I read *The Stand*. Broke my heart. I had never hurt like that before. There were things that hurt me, but not in that way. Not in the way one aches for the well-being of strangers. Not in that helpless way it breaks when there is no compromise, no saving, no helping, and no praying that will make anything better—when the story has long been finished and the storyteller cannot be moved to change the ending to spare your feelings. That special kind of heartbreak that authors know exist in the compassion we, as humans, are able to feel for people we don't and can't ever know—Thank you Tolkien, for reopening that wound about a year later.

The Road by Cormac McCarthy has become almost a bible to me. In fact, it's the only book I've kept. I would have liked to keep more. I feel like I have abandoned friends, or at least, people who have done good things for me or effected my life, in a good way.

But *The Road* gives me a sense of not being alone in this. Even before the dead revolted, the book filled a void where faith in parents and family should have been. It made me wish I had a father like "the man". *Anyone* like him… Since all this started, that fictional father has been this real woman's mentor. More so, it makes me appreciate my circumstances in this life and before. Most importantly, it made—and makes—me hopeful that there are good people in the world.

It gave and gives me hope.
And now I have the time to read it as often as I please.
There aren't a lot of authors like McCarthy anymore, if there ever were. If he's alive, I'd love to know what this situation stirs in that brilliant mind—and hope he is well.

I hope you are well.

Video games and books particularly impact me, because you spend more time with the characters than in movies. Sometimes TV series have characters I've liked that much—but <u>few</u>. A lot of series, I think, ruin the characters when the stories last longer than their stories and the inspiration behind them, just because they are popular.

For me—I know that's not true for everybody.

Video games, most of the time, you're getting someone's story too, BUT you're fighting beside them, keeping them safe and "helping" the characters make their decisions.

I know that won't ring true for people who think video games are a waste of time or for people who just don't get into it, but I'd love to know I'm not the only one that was horrified when Agro died in *Shadow of the Colossus* or that cried themselves sick through the last battle in *God of War* where Kratos had to desperately hold onto his family to win.

Maybe I *am* the only one, now.

Anyway, it's those things I miss and, on top of the people I loved and knew well, were a whole shitload of people I *didn't* know—maybe even their names—whose work made my life better.

I think about what's become of them. I could fill these pages with just the names of people that I hate to think of gone. My writer's callous would look like a chopstick rest. :)
It's not really a writer's callous, but maybe a "drawer's". I like drawing. It helps me arrange my thoughts.

I bet you could fill a book too, if you thought about all the people that affect your life in a good way… even if he or she only wrote one song that always makes you smile. There are a lot of people involved in your life.

I was a waitress and I got treated like shit by people who thought I was nothing, but demanded the best of me. I always wanted to point out, "You know, this isn't my dream job." But they wouldn't care.

Someone has to do the jobs we don't want to do. Those people should be respected more, not less, for doing those things. But, since that's not the way the world works, you just smile and resist the urge to pop their self-important bubble—and spend the hours wishing that zombies would just kill everybody.

There are only a couple people, who come to mind, that I *still* think I would be more than happy to know they were dead or died badly.

Again, automatically, the first thing that comes to mind is: Is Akira Yamoaka okay? Howard Shore? Hans Zimmer? Laura Linney? The really nice lady at the grocery who always asks me how I am? My friends…

I'm grieving. I'm wondering, worrying. I hope when I can, as much as I can.

That's not even the weird stuff that I end up thinking about. I don't think that's weird at all. Its compassion, isn't it?

Maybe compassion is weird. It was before, why wouldn't it be now?

Oct 3 10:02am

On the right day, when the wind is coming from someplace better than here, I smell the air the way it used to be.

That's about the time when Mr. Ages will come and put his head on my knee, panting happily, maybe wondering why I'm not as tense—then I smell his stinking breath.

I pick him over for ticks and hate his dense wavy fur. If I miss one, it swells and gets gray and shiny. One of my friends is a criminal psychologist and lives near Duluth. There was a ritual in her family for when ticks were found on people. After they were pulled off, her folks always put matches to them in her dad's brown ashtray. They would get puffy, like Corn Nuts. Sometimes they would pop, I think that was the goal, but maybe it was just to make them round and hard like that. I think her folks probably only meant to kill them, but it was something she remembers fondly.

One thing I remember fondly, was the bear ashtray with the rocks and the small pool where ashes would be tapped into. There was a small fish in the pool. The whole piece was glazed and very shiny. I remember petting the fish and wondering, if it every broke off, if they would let me keep it.

I fondly remember the homemade birthday cakes and pumpkin bars with raisins her mother used to make. If you got them straight out of the oven, the raisins were SO warm and juicy. When they were cool, her mom would put cream cheese frosting on them. I was greedy when I visited Dee. I was also ashamed of myself. I was embarrassed of my life.

I don't know what state you're in—

If you're reading this sometime after this shit, maybe you are glad to have dates and/or times. If you're reading this sometime after this shit, you could be an alien. Do dates and times mean anything to you?

I'm sure most of us can't help but let these little things go. There's so much else to worry about, why keep time?

Time, I suppose, will take a hike when the battery in my watch dies.

To keep the days—it's such a little thing, why stop?

So we give up one thing here and one little thing there—I'm afraid of what that adds up to.

Besides, how can any of us think that each day doesn't mean a hell of a lot more now than it did before??? Corita Kent said:

"Life is a succession of moments. To live each one is to succeed."

It's been about 120 days. That feels pretty significant. Each entry is significant. I'm lucky.

You are lucky too.

-

There's this busy body I see almost every day that I haven't "killed." I think it's because I can't stand to get near him—not that I want to get near any of them.

He was my mailman—he was a creep before.

Something ate most of his lower face, but didn't want to eat his Droopy lips—they just hang between cheeks, and those almost look like saggy butt cheeks and—they always reminded me of that cartoon dog, Droopy.

Did it disgust anyone but me that, in the cartoon, humans were attracted to that? Maybe you don't know.

Am I giving away my age?

So violent music and video games desensitize people to violence, supposedly, right?

What the fuck did all those moments in cartoon history do to the children watching animals getting romantic with "sexy" human women? That insurance commercial with the pig that ends up with the guy's girlfriend did that too.

And shooter video games are a problem?

There were a lot of things wrong with the way things were.

I've thought a lot about why this is happening—obviously settling on the parasite idea, but that's mainly because it's a lot more comfortable to think about than the most realistic explanation I thought of...

You know how places introduce species into an environment to get rid of pests or other problems? I'm almost too afraid to think that God might be doing that to us. How else do the dead come back? For all my life, if someone asked, do I believe in life after death I'd say "yes," one way or another.

One way or another.

For people who aren't even agnostic—this all must be a hell of a thing to digest. How? How? How? How? How? *How?*

Why?

I guess because of heavy metal and furries.
I guess it doesn't matter.
They are.
There's no denying that.

I wonder if anyone has taken shelter in my house. Are they dead? Did they face what I escaped?

Are they wondering about the freak that lived there? ☺

I almost didn't survive my first night in *this* house.

...it was good that it was too big to fit under the bed. It was good that it was "fresh" enough that it couldn't just crawl out of its flesh and get under. Lord knows it tried.

And it was good that the owner of this house had lamps that make pretty damn good clubs.

Right now isn't the best time for that story.

Oct 4 1:55pm

I've been avoiding an issue.
Winter is coming.

I told myself that it's going to slow them down—maybe even stop them when it's below freezing…

…but it's going to stop me too.

I don't have supplies for winter.

I don't have supplies for a month.

And I'm afraid.

2:02pm

What's out there?

Oct 5 9:20am

Hi—How are you?

I wish we could compare notes.

As an end of the world, post-apocalypse movies and books junkie, I asked myself a million times before, what would I do? What would I do if there were zombies? What would I do if I woke up and I was alone in the world?

I would *always* be excited.

I would go to stores and get anything I wanted and food would never spoil—or at least it never seemed to be a problem. No stress. No worries. No work—no bosses. No bills.

I was excited, like it would solve all my problems.

When it really happened, it wasn't quite like that.

Zombie movies gave me some ideas about what I could do. But having skills would help.

This shit is the kind of thing I fantasized about when I thought I'd never get out of my stupid ass job.

Well, zombies would certainly put an end that- Ha! Ha! Ha!

A zombie apocalypse actually felt more likely than getting out of my job had.

I couldn't get through a day of work without getting *Grief*, by Dir en Grey, in my head. If you know the song, you'd completely understand.

My friend, the psychologist, would have bad days and always get *My Immortal* by Evanescence in her head. I think largely because of the first line. Now, I'm tired of being here, too. Okay. Supplies.

I have some dog food and treats. Some flour and sugar and rice. There are a few more cans of veggies—yuck.

Under normal circumstances, I really only enjoy frozen or fresh vegetables. One fruit cocktail. If ever I get bit, that's going to be my last meal. I hope it has lots of cherries and pineapple— but I swear they're mostly pears and grapes.

The bath tub is about ¼ full of water that I ran out of the pipes—that's all the drinking water I have. Sometimes I stand in the room and stare at it… looking at it as measurements of gallons, quarts, cups… estimating, planning… sometimes just checking to make sure it's still there.

Technically the creek is fresh water, but I am wary of drinking from it. I think of the condition of the water they tolerated drinking in *The Road* and it makes me feel stuck-up to turn up my nose at "fresh water", but I'm afraid. I have no one to look after me. There's no one to help if I get sick. I think about parasites. I think about bloated corpses growing rancid as they decay somewhere upstream.

I-don't-want-to-get-sick.

I just can't take the chance.

Winter is undoable here.

I only made it *this* far on my first try at supplies. I'm still on the same fucking road.

Damn it.

Oct 6 12:25pm

How did this nightmare begin?
I was heading home.
I had about 8 ½ hours of driving left.

Okay, let me back up… to where it started…
I was on vacation, in South Dakota, with my best friends.
We'd been at the resort for a week—really secluded—so we could catch up on a whole lot of years that were sewn together by, now, infrequent phone calls, some letters and plenty of emails.

We left our cars about a mile away—closer to ¾ a mile—to hike to our cabin.

It was so private we didn't know. We had no idea.

We requested the most isolated cabin at the resort—so there were a lot of things we just didn't see. We were drinking, carousing, carrying on while the world was ending, but I'm getting ahead of myself.

One of my friends' husbands called at one point and was as clear about vague news broadcasts as he could be. Weird things in newspapers and word of mouth. Really weird things online. The word "hoax" came up. War of the Worlds—that kinda b.s.

Something weird was going on—he couldn't wait until she got home.

That was that.

My other friends turned off their phones when we first arrived and didn't think a lot about them. We were supposed to. Complete social blackout. This was about us.

We didn't think much of hearing screams around a lake. There seemed to be a lot of helicopters. But what would we know? There was an abundance of sirens throughout each day, but accidents happen. There'd be lots of reasons for that. Campfires, boating accidents, drunks, fights, break-ins, heart attacks. Things happen.

But what we could not see and couldn't understand then, is terrifying in retrospect—in understanding. Like reaching under your car seat for the keys you dropped and finding out later there had been a poisonous snake under it.

We didn't know people were leaving. The people who owned the resort had their own things to worry about.

Night five of six—suddenly seemed like *a lot* of sirens out there. That and the perpetual pounding of helicopter propellers.

Something really bad must have happened.

My heart responded to the unknown tragedy. I remember the skin prickling on the back of my neck.

I was alone then, my friend Dee having crawled to bed sometime after 11:30. We were all exhausted from a week of the antics of longtime friends, so 11:30 felt pretty late.

Dee and I'd been up reminiscing—and catching up on our latest horror movie discoveries—she being every bit the horror addict as me. She ~~was~~ *is*. We also bond over our love of Japanese music, especially Visual Kei.

Above any of my friends, I often felt we were too close to be anything but sisters. I always wished we were.

Everything about that night is still so clear in my mind.

I rose, feeling dread creeping up on me like a shy psychic vision. I went quietly, out into the night. The air was cold against my arms and legs. Inside, my skin was getting clammy from this growing sense of danger. For some reason, I felt that if I came out here, if I looked, I could see it coming… whatever it was.

I reached out with my left hand, the right occupied with a drink. The wooden rail, needing some tlc, clung to some of the warmth it drank from the day. Sunlight only ever hit the front of the cabin. The trees gathered close, and their reach was almost as great as the needled limbs stretching out of them.

I was on the deck, listening to drone of sirens and loons on the lake—their "meh-no-biggie-super-familiar" song sounded eerie that night. The muscles in my legs went cold. My knees loosened—I don't know if they wanted to buckle or move me.

The soda in my hand was sweating.

My mouth was dry when nearer sirens woke me, so I grabbed it from the fridge before I came out.

There was a chill, wasn't there? Maybe it was me.

The cabin was dark behind me. The woods were tall and black. The shadows, stubborn and ungiving. The moon was bright, but it still had a couple of days to fullness. And still, for all the trees, there was only light where I stood. I felt, not that something in it, but the dark itself was watching me.

I sensed my friends were awake, but lying still in their beds, probably thinking the same thing I was about the sirens. Inside, where they lay, on their sides, facing windows…eyes staring—and burning from not blinking.

Why hadn't the sirens stopped?

Before then, I was perfectly comfortable on the deck of that unfamiliar building, in those unfamiliar woods, in the dark, in the middle of the night. Anything could have been with me. *Anything* could have been out there. That Anything could have been watching me. Sneaking up on me.

I felt like something was.

My watch face lit up in blue-green light and read 12:47.

I would never feel safe at night again.

That was the last time I'd ever stand outside and not question what was "out there." Soon, I'd be worried about what was hiding "in there" too.

I closed the screen door and swung the hook into the elbow of a bent nail that married the door to its frame.

The humidity was unforgiving, even at night, and we had not locked or even closed the inside door since we first unlocked it.

That night I closed it. Then I locked it.

All those sirens—there could be a manhunt going on, after all—and that's what I told myself.

I closed the curtains and checked them—I closed the ones that were open and locked all the windows on the first floor.

I sat down on the couch. I sipped my drink—the bubbles tingled against my lips and the carbonation sounded urgent against the roof of my mouth. I sat the bottle on a magazine on the coffee table. I can't remember who was on the cover.

I've thought about that Dr. Pepper a lot since then.

I laid down on the couch and watched heavy beads of moisture gather and run on the sweating plastic.

I dream of that.

Straining for the slightest creak or rustle, my ears began to ring until I could barely concentrate on anything else. It's the kind of hard listening that requires the eyes to strain themselves. As when you stare into the dark, afraid, until your eyes burn and run with tears intended to moisten them… the kind of searching and staring that demands your ears come off the pillow and paralyzes your being, that your sheets and clothes lay silently across you. Their rustling is too loud.

My neck began to hurt. I let me head down to the throw pillow that lay between it and my bent arm. I couldn't see that I would be able to sleep. The hour just turned when I thought I'd rest my eyes:

It was 1am.

-

I woke up to the sound of the toaster announcing the end of its cycle. I heard my friends talking—minus Dee, who I'd shortly find out was still sleeping. Big surprise. Dee's definitely a 12 hour sleeper. I am more of a 5—THANK GOD!

I smelled coffee brewing. It was just starting to "fart"—that's what Marie called it:

"Man in the Bathroom"

Tinkle, tinkle, tinkle—fart, fart… silence.

It's our last full day—let's hit the lake, they said.

I'm not a fan of deep water, but a five year reunion is no place to say, "I don't want to do that with you."

I remember the clock on the microwave, the bright red digital numerals blazing out of its rectangular, cave-like face. I remember watching 6:04, 6:05, 6:06 come and go. Next to me Lindsay was telling a joke. I didn't hear a word, but her tone. And then I was enveloped in the sound of their laughter—Marie's being the greatest, both in volume and contagiousness.

Above us, Dee was stirring. I heard the bed first, then the crude delivery of her sock-warmed feet to the wood floor. How long would she sit there—eyes closed like a lizard on a rock, privately cursing us out and wondering what she'd done wrong to deserve seeing this hour? Arms heavy, she would stand and have to decide to come down as is or change her clothes. I heard her move to the stairs. She was wearing yesterdays' clothes and didn't give a damn. I pulled my eyes off the time and looked at the lot of us. None of us had changed. If we'd had to rush out in the middle of the night, we would have been dressed for it.

I wonder if that was incidental…

We carried our coffee to the rowboat and took turns with the oars. The lake had a thin mist on it that matched the steam coming off our drinks.

Our talk that morning was the kind I yearn for—talk that matters. This was when we revealed our current *real* problems, fears—what was hurting us. Everything serious had been really intermittent and casually addressed up until this point—our conversations had been fueled by our excitement of being back together. We nonchalantly asked of marital and financial problems, of worries and stubborn personal issues, like if Carrie had finally quit smoking.

When we talk, like we talked that morning—inevitably, we're all crying—then one of us, usually Marie, just laughs for "no reason" and then we all laugh or someone says something stupid and it's done.

In my memory, it felt like something we *had* to do, because we knew we wouldn't get another chance.

We didn't bring up how quiet it was on the lake. No boats. No more distant yelling. No more screams. But there were regular helicopters passing over.

There were more sirens.

And something just didn't feel right.

If you can, imagine sitting on a lake and having a premonition there was going to be a nuclear strike—somewhere near enough that you would see the mushroom cloud—that's what we were feeling.

At least I was.

Something climbed aboard that boat and that horrible, unsettling thing embraced us. It draped across us, even as we planned a crazy last night with forced enthusiasm.

Conversation even felt obligatory.

I made myself be the way I felt I should be.
Being a waitress, I was good at that.
But the two of my friends who were moms…their eyes were devouring invisible miles—looking for their kids.
Dee just looked troubled—there was flatness in her eyes.
Everything inside her perfectly cautious mind was preoccupied.

Something was gnawing at my insides. I had an urgent need to be moving—anywhere, somewhere—to someplace familiar… to get my ass home.

It was about 9pm when we—first Lindsay—asked what the point would be to spend one more night since we all had to get up so early the next day. We might as well get a head start and see the next morning through our own home's windows.

We all had a supporting reason to end our reunion early. I said there were a lot of things I'd put off at the house and, since this was the last of my vacation time, it'd be nice to have a day to catch up.

No one was disappointed that the others were agreeing to cut it short. It seemed we were relieved. We didn't even care about paying for a day we wouldn't be there. I was never in a habit of throwing away money. I loathed to rent or go to movies because you walk away with nothing but an experience. I always waited to buy and own that experience—cheap.

So not using that time should have really bothered me, but it didn't. I didn't give one shit about it or leaving all our groceries behind. I didn't give it a thought, until weeks later.

All that seemed to matter, to each of us, was to get home. There was a sense that we all needed to go back to "START", before whatever we were afraid of started.

Carrie lived closest, about an hour away.

I had a 12 ½ hour drive ahead…

Dee was going to see about changing her ticket to an earlier flight—she flew because she couldn't spare the hours on roundtrip driving. Not with her professional responsibilities. I had offered to pick her up, but she felt bad. That would be out of my way.

Always considerate. *Always.*

The others were somewhere in between those hours, going north or south or west. I doubt I'll ever never know where they ended up.

The resort office was open—the lights were on, anyway.

Marie went in and told them we were leaving. When she came out, she casually told us that the lady who ran the place, with her husband, thought we were already gone—even though our vehicles were there.

We started saying our goodbye's. I threw out a few, I felt necessary, jabs at my friends—the friendly, jack-assed kind—then the lady who owned the resort stepped out onto the office steps.

She looked horrible. Half dead. I'm guessing Marie thought, maybe hoped, we'd never see her.

"Good luck," the woman said sincerely—and gravely, I felt. She said it like she meant it, like she knew the consequences of "no luck".

I caught a glimpse of her husband, Chuck, when she went inside. He had a kitchen towel over one of his huge, thick hands. There was blood on the towel—a crescent moon was cut into the fatty ball of flesh under his thumb knuckle—like he had cut himself on a glass.

But we both know it wasn't glass, right?

I think I knew it then, but it was too weird to recognize or acknowledge.

I felt like crying and puking as I chucked my stuff in the trunk. I remember my hands were trembling. All of me was trembling, but my quaking hands were making it hard to function… and they were giving away what I was feeling.

My hands and arms felt cold and a little numb. I barely felt my purse, when I opened the driver's side door just enough to toss it to the front passenger seat. I closed the door with the weight of my body. I didn't want to face the others.

I don't know why or how, but I knew this was a goodbye like those given over a life support machine—when it's about to be shut off. Every molecule of my being screamed that these faces I loved, I would never see again. That these voices and laughs might never be heard again, but in my memory. My soul was delivered the bad news, but at the time I just didn't know why I was despairing like that…why any of us were.

I was waving to my friends and we were calling out goodbyes and smiling. I didn't have to force any of this.

Then I watched their taillights come on and I followed them out. I was behind Lindsay until the first highway entrance. My heart pinched. It wrung. It shriveled. It bled. It knew what I didn't know. Watch animals when something bad is going to happen, when there is a storm, for instance. They flee, hide, prepare—they react long before we smell rain. Maybe with something this big, even our undeveloped perceptions pick up on the signal to run for higher land…just like rats.

I watched her lights until they disappeared. There was no one behind me to annoy. Then it was me and the road and a shitload of dark. That's when I remembered I'd left my Dr. Pepper on the coffee table. I had the strangest impulse to go back for it. I ignored it.

In my chest was the sound of a billiard ball rolling back and forth—the sound of it hitting the inside a box. My shoulders heaved—my breaths were too big. I was fighting something, myself—sorrow, grief, fear… I don't know. But it was huge. I felt like a werewolf, refusing its transformation. I felt like screaming. I threw my head back and took a deep breath instead. I feel so fucked up sometimes, like a vase that's been broken and fixed so many times that its shape has changed and the pictures are stretched out by the glue that binds the pieces… I got angry at myself. I despair so easily… I imagine the worst. I know me. I dread things. I reminded myself of myself. Told myself to drive and that everything was fine, as it usually was. Ignoring a tiny voice inside me declaring good reason for being this way, I turned east and started home.

It didn't surprise me to see vehicles cruising around during bar hours. I didn't know what to think of how many I saw, because I wasn't local. It was June—vacationers everywhere.

But the traffic stayed busy and naturally worsened when I skimmed the city limits of a larger town—there were a lot of police cars. A few military vehicles. A number of civilian vehicles on the side of the road. Some wrecks. I just thought, "Asshole drivers." Impatient, probably. Like there's somewhere to go that's more important than your life, or anyone elses'.

In hindsight, there were a lot of indications of what was really wrong and how bad it was. I just couldn't see and I *wouldn't* see until I was forced to deal with a situation head on. *Then* I *saw*.

But that was later.

At that time, I was more concerned with dealing with the hours on the road and wishing Dee was making the trip with me. This is a wish I wished again and again. A wish I'm wishing now...

I never count on finding channels with enough music I like to bother listening to the radio. So, like on the way there, I was listening to my MP3 player and didn't think about checking news—maybe I wasn't concerned about hearing it, I can't remember.

The first song that played, *Embryo* by Dir en Grey, seeped almost more from the dark than from my speakers when it started. When I love a song, it's almost parasitic—I let the music take me, sink its teeth in. I let the song devour me. Sometimes it feels good to put in the earbuds, spread out on a bed or the carpet and be eclipsed in a perfect song.

In this case, the songs were eating the miles and I was gladly losing time.

Later, my cell phone rang once, but the bars were low and the sounds I got didn't add up to words. It was Marie.
I saw I was at about ½ a tank and was compelled to top off.

That probably had less to do with some intuitive fear of whatever bad thing I was sensing, than just knowing I was crossing South Dakota and I sure as hell didn't want to run out of gas between towns... in the middle of the night.

The service station was busy and I had to wait behind four other vehicles for my turn.

Out in the orange lights of the Cenex, everyone was talking excitedly—no, *hysterically*.

I wanted a cold drink, so after I filled up I went inside. The shelves were nearly picked clean. There were no drinks to buy, but people weren't ravaging the "to-go" food as badly—so I "settled for" a 32 oz. vanilla soft serve with a straw and paid for my gas. I didn't take all I could of the goods there. I didn't even buy chips.

The young clerk looked exhausted or scared.
When I checked out we shared a look of confusion.
"Anything else?" she said.

Behind me someone said something about "...nurses treating people on the sidewalks."

At the next register someone was buying a spare gas can. Its redness seemed brilliant. Beckoning. My ears were ringing. I felt like they were going underwater. I couldn't stop looking at it.

I told her "no" and goodnight.

At 1:21am

I left into the less stuffy sound of the same conversations, but outdoors. You'd have thought everyone knew each other because they were talking so urgently, loudly, prattling off news and about places they'd been and where they were going.

Outside, I was able to free my attention from that gas can, but then I saw red—EVERYWHERE. The one inside might have been the last. It looked like the rest were out here. Some people even had 3 or 4 of them. Made me wonder if I wouldn't be wise to follow suit, but I just wanted to get away from there.

Three people were looking through the windows on the opposite side of my car. They barely hid their guilt enough to move a couple steps back, as I approached.

I used my key (because I always lock my car doors—even if I step away for only a couple minutes) and entered through the passenger side. I wasn't going to stand in the middle of them with my purse and keys in hand.

I was nervous to slide into the driver's seat. I didn't want to make eye contact, but I kept them in my peripheral vision as much as I could. I only looked down long enough to slip my key in the ignition. When I looked up I noticed all the out of state plates.

I reminded myself, who was I to know what could be going on that they would be there. I didn't know. Actually, they couldn't have known yet either—or at least the magnitude of it all or I'm sure most those travelers wouldn't have bothered to be as "civil" as they were.

I didn't overlook the fear and confusion in most faces. I didn't overlook that every vehicle was packed to the roof, either.

I turned the key and crept through the disorderly gas station. People were yelling at me and everyone else at the pumps, impatient for their turn. Out of the corner of my eye, I saw the people surge on what looked like a fight that had broken out inside the station. Someone ran with a gun. Something told me I needed to get the hell out of there. I switched on the blinker, turning east. I looked both ways and then up at nothing—because I was listening. I slightly tilted my head toward my left shoulder and squinted—as if that actually helps, but I didn't hear it again.

I thought I heard a gunshot.

After waiting for a few vehicles to pass, I turned out, glancing at the car's clock:

1:26am

I was worried. *Beyond* instinct—I really *knew* I should be.
I wondered where my friends were.
I started thinking about family I hadn't seen since I was a child.

It was a little further down the road when I found out that worry was too small a word for the concern I should be feeling for my friends. Everything before was like a tornado watch. *It* was a warning. Then, I had every reason to be scared for my life. All lives.

It was horrible and unreal.

At first it wasn't horrible—I can't describe it. I think that's just not the right word.

In a dream everything is possible. Sometimes you wake up and you're in a heightened state of fear—it was *that* fear, plus the mortal panic of seeing something ethereal—like facing God, but with the exact opposite energy that I think a person would feel in God's presence. If you believe we're not always in it.

I can't describe it.

Damn it.
It's like my soul was terrified.
My soul. Jesus.

In *Home Alone*, Kevin wishes his family would disappear.
I fantasized so many times about this happening.

Sometimes I yearned for it—I <u>wished it</u> with <u>absolute</u> sincerity. No bullshitting—I WANTED THIS.

I can't even address that part of me—it's sitting in my mental "IN" box.

Should I feel guilt? I suppose I should feel satisfied? I don't—I just don't want to go there.

Anyway—I just thought about that.

I made my family disappear.

If I leave this house will I end up a long ways from here? ~~Will I see one of my friends' cars on the vehicle graveyard interstate?~~

Or maybe my doctors will find the right combination of medications and I'll come to in a mental hospital and everyone will be okay. Will always have been okay… as okay as we were.

It's just any other day, before the impossible happens.

That's how it always is in movies and, sadly, in reality, a good deal of the time too.

Everything is routine until aliens show up.

I feel so bad.

I never have things happen that I want or think that I want.

Sometimes I felt like fate was against me for how much bad luck I've had. I used to say, "Do I stink? I should. I've been pissed on all day."

That my simple escapist fantasy could be responsible for this and my unlikely survival. At least I can't know if it was me or any other person out there who wondered what it would be like.

Believe me, I'm not the only one.

Anyone who was tired of the routine and dreaming of something more exciting in their life… If they're dead and I'm not, should I blame myself? I dunno. I can't stop picking this scab.

God, it's late. I'll run down batteries and this is definitely not worth it. Maybe I'll finish this story another time…

Oct 12 12:55pm

I wish you could tell me how this happened for you.

Oct 17 11:15am

Mr. Ages looks like he's laughing on mute. I love his face.

I've never had a pet before. He's more like a companion, I guess. I don't think of him as a pet… Do I? I don't know what to think of him. But I love his face and I need his presence. He is basking in the sun and those dark eyes are sparkly wet and the heat has put that smile on his face, and the bead of drool, hanging heavily, on the round end of his tongue.

I know he's overheating, but he looks so happy.

The long and wavy pile of his coat is getting oily. Its true color is dulled by the grime we are each becoming more and more accustomed to. I hope that's a symptom of conditioning rather than of a slow drain on my give-a-damn.

The trees are amazing. The maples appear to be burning, the same way that the sun set fire to the fox. The thin leaves drink the light like lampshades… awakening the brilliant color lying dormant there. They dance like flames in the breeze. The wind is warm—unseasonably? I wouldn't know, but it feels amazing.

The air smells so sweet—strange how all these dying things smell so good.

The leaves aren't crunchy, but soft with dew. There's about four inches of leaves on top of more than a foot of browning grass. In the morning I can walk silently across it. Dawn and dusk eat into more and more of the day…stretching the night between them…

It's almost Halloween. I'm pretty sure it won't be the same thing this year. I'm almost afraid of what will happen.

It could make things worse. Who knows?

I love Halloween.

I used to work really hard to spend most of it scared out of my mind—with Dee's help. She would always visit to celebrate the holiday, her favorite too. She said I had a better yard for the haunted cemetery we raised every year. But I think she also liked to go somewhere she didn't have to lift a finger for a few days.

I'd go to her place over our birthdays—mine's January 17th and hers, the 21st. Since we met, when we were 9, I've spent every birthday with her.

Are you alone?

Is it not enormously stupid to ask you questions? A perpetual or paradoxical question in itself, isn't it?

Is it not enormously stupid to be curious about you?
Maybe not. The world has become a place of questions. And, unless you supply them yourself, there won't be any answers.

Oct 18 9:30am

I found the road map—I knew I had one; I just had it in a different spot. ~~I must have been organizing~~ It was still in my "flee" pack.

I know I have to head south. How far?
Am I looking for other people or just warmer weather? There have got to be other people out there, but do I want to cross paths with them?
I know how it is here.
I don't know anything else.
All I know, and all I keep thinking, is that when I tried to go anywhere before I didn't make it <u>five</u> miles!

Should I try to find my friends first?

I can't know if anyone's okay.

Do I dare leave?

What if someone comes looking for me?

I'm not even at *my* house. Why would anyone think I'd still be there? Could they believe I made it back to Wisconsin? No one would look for me here… no one would look for me. It would be stupid for me to look for them. How deeply I crave answers, on the condition that the answer is good news… how terribly I dread ever knowing any one person I love is gone—or imagining how. Or knowing how.

I need to start addressing my own fate. Winter has announced herself… she does so with small cold bites. I don't see that I can survive more than that.

I just don't have any idea what I'm going to do.

This won't hold out.

But damn—it's beautiful right now.

Oct 19 3:11pm

Just washed up at the creek—water's getting cold.

I contemplate cutting my hair off. It's very long. Probably dangerously long, literally. I had a busy body get a hold of it once, I should have probably cut it off then… but, *he* liked it.

When I brush it out I can almost feel him run his fingers through it. He would braid it while we watch movies; I'd sit in front of him. ~~We~~

Mr. Ages is a mess, but he's happy.

He killed a huge squirrel earlier. He'll miss the frogs. He ate a lot of them. They did hellable things to his breath, but he was fed and that made me feel good. I'm all out of dog food.
Cripes, that's a whole other can of worms.
How do I travel with Bark Face?
I'm not leaving him.

But that also sounds like certain death.

He won't do a muzzle. I don't have a real one, and the ones I've invented, he's gotten off and hated until he did.
I'll have to see if I can find one—I doubt a lot of pet supply shops were over picked over, yet.

I've never muzzled a dog.
Can they still make a sound?
I know I don't want him biting anything.

If something happens to me—he can't be stuck in a muzzle.

Anyway, was also going to tell you that I got two more: Turtle
and a stranger. I hate strangers...
I thought the mailman might have turned in his chips,
somewhere. But there the fucker is right now.
Wait a minute Mr. Postman. Got something to do.

I brought Mr. Ages inside.
I couldn't find that damn busy body.
If I can get the nerve to face him, I can handle
anything.
There *are* freakier busy bodies, but there are
no creepier ones.
When a creep's job is to know where you live
it makes him ten times the creepy.

-

I can't figure out if I'm writing this to you or for me.

-

I have to minimize.

I liked to collect things. Little things that made me happy to
have them. Just to look at. No real purpose, but they brought
me pleasure.
I can't do that anymore. Practicality is a tyrant... and will beat
out whatever joy a person can find.

People lock their doors to keep their things safe when they're away. It makes me sick to think of someone ransacking my life for something useful and tossing aside things that mattered so much to me.

I never meant to leave them.

I didn't know I wouldn't be going back.

But I always have, on me, the things that I <u>can't</u> leave—except when I'm washing up, but I keep those things nearby.

I'm looking at a picture of my grandma. I'm a baby and she's holding me. The back says I'm a month old. She must have only been in her sixties, but she looks twenty years older than that, to me.

I don't think she was ever young.

My fingertips drift over the white edges of the photographs pinned between my folded legs. They feel like playing cards and make a sound like them when the roughness of my thumb drags across them. For fractions of seconds, fragments of my past, captured therein, flicker before me. The whiteness of smiles, the reddish blur of a bad exposure or radial glow of a lens flare… the blue of a sky. Every one of them a moment captured for a reason… from an age when no one had photo printers in their homes and digital cameras were a pipedream. Photos weren't as arbitrary.

Someone else would just throw these pictures away.

-

Anyway, I guess I never finished telling you what happened to me on the way home from the reunion with my friends.

Like I was saying, I probably would have known what was going on sooner if I hadn't been where I was at the time—there were vehicles, but not a lot of towns between the resort and Rhinelander. It was night, during most of my trip to and from the resort. On the way out west, I remember the towns gravely still, like I was the only person awake to see the hours.

I owned the night.

On my way back, there were more lights. In the dark, it seemed like the shadows were squirming.

I didn't keep track of how many times I pulled over for emergency vehicles to pass—it was a lot. The first time was the worst and, that time only, flashing lights weren't only to get me out of the way.

I have been pulled over twice in my whole life.

Ever since I was little, I've felt guilty. I felt guilty I had to be fed. I felt guilty I was using up shampoo or toothpaste. I felt guilty because Jesus died for me. I felt guilty when I needed to go to the dentist or eye doctor because I knew my parents were reluctant to take me. One time, I'm sure I broke a rib and I told my dad that I hurt. He sighed and said, "son-of-a-*bitch*" then looked at me—something intolerant, hateful blazed in his eyes.

He said, "Well, if you're not better in a couple weeks I guess we'll have to take you to a doctor."

I never brought it up again.

Once, after church—I would have been six or seven—we had to stop for gas. It was full service and my mom (dad never went to church) told the boy, "Twenty dollars." When she took out the bill she smoothed it and held it up and stared at it and—just like dad did—sighed hugely, unignorably, as she reluctantly passed it off. Something made me feel responsible for her having to spend that twenty-dollars.

I heard the same sigh when I needed things for school—every year—especially if I outgrew my coat or shoes. I fell in love with thrift shops, at first out of obligation, because that cut down on a lot of sighs that were my fault. Everything seemed to be my fault. I swear, the mortgage bill would come and they'd be furious at me.

I cannot conjure the sound of their voices without the stiffness of irritation. Barely did I even hear *that* voice compared to all of the yelling...

One of my earliest memories, or senses of reality, was feeling I'd done something wrong.

In my home, there was no such thing as a little anger—any little thing, from the smallest disagreement to something being out of place was met with *rage*. There was no such thing as sorry. It was terrifying. I walked on eggshells for seventeen years.

A lot of kids wore hand-me-downs from their brothers or sisters. I wore hand-me-downs from my parents.

I never complained. I didn't complain, until now, I guess.

I tried to be good.

My existence was inconvenient—I became apologetic for everything. Nervous about everything.

I didn't have a strong sense of self value. Maybe <u>any</u> sense. And my minister said that Jesus died for <u>me</u>??

I didn't feel like I was worth anything… that really made me feel like shit.

So, many years later, when I was first pulled over, because I had a taillight out—I was sick with fear that I'd done something terribly wrong, but I just didn't know I had.

Are you still with me?

So it was June, on the road between Hill City, South Dakota and Rhinelander, Wisconsin. My home.

The red and blues lit up my car for the first of many times that night:

It was 2:02am

8 ½ hours from home.

Lindsay always told me that you ask a cop to show you their badge before you roll down your window, to make sure they really are a cop. I considered that both times when I'd been pulled over.

I couldn't. Complacent was my nature.

When exactly do they consider something like that obstruction? Would they be good natured about it?
Would they understand that people can be evil and, it wouldn't be the first time a monster took advantage of someone via a costume and novelty lights?

I thought it would take a minute for them to get out, because I assume they always run tags and plates or whatever, but it only took a sec before I saw his silhouette cut into the strobing lights.

I turned on my interior lights, rolled down my window and waited—because I read somewhere that you should do that for police. They don't exactly have the nicest job. Every time they approach someone they are taking a chance.

"Where are you headed?" he asked. He was a state trooper. I thought I would remember his name, but I can't. Maybe later.

I told him, "Wisconsin."

"Well you can't go this way."
I picked up my Google maps print out as if it would show me alternate routes.
I was about to ask why.
"You don't want to go this way," he amended.

"Okay," I agreed—I was okay to change my route—something was wrong in town. Fine. "How do I reconnect with this road?"
"Have a road map?"
"Not of South Dakota," I said. "I haven't left Wisconsin in years."

That wasn't exactly true, but my out of state trips were to places I knew by heart and didn't need a map.

He sighed. In a nice way.
He pulled out his ticket book and wrote on it for a moment.
Then he gave me the directions I hoped he was writing.
I thanked him and told him how much I appreciated that.

"Sure thing," he said in an easy way.

Headlights appeared some distance off in my rear view. He noticed too. Time to go.

"Well I hope they open up the roads for you soon," I said.

The faintest line appeared between his eyebrows and vanished as quick. I didn't understand what the look meant, yet. I assume he wondered if I knew about *them* or not.

He waited in front of his headlights until I took the left turn that his directions said. By then, the other car was getting close. He'd be dealing with them soon.

I felt uncomfortable on that old county road. Though tar and perfectly maintained, it had an abandoned feel. I had the sense I was purposely misguided, like in The Hills Have Eyes.

I was some distance on the detour when suddenly I had to swerve for a suitcase and braked for the car that birthed it.

Luggage and their contents were strewn over about 15 feet of road. There were a few totes, haphazard and spewing. The lid for one was in the ditch, illuminated by my headlights. The station wagon's gate was open into the left lane.

I didn't want to run over someone's things.

I didn't want to go out in the dark—especially because it didn't look safe. It looked ransacked, robbed. Where were the people who were in it before? They didn't run out of gas—most people, I think, actually make it to the side of the road. I took out my cell phone. Only a tiny bar pulsed. I dialed 9-1-1.

When my signal held long enough to ring, a computer told me that all available dispatchers were on other calls—blah, blah, blah.

I swore and thought about going back and seeing if I could find the officer again, but what if someone was hurt?
I couldn't see around the vehicle—there might be another vehicle. I don't know anything about medicine, but I thought I might have been able to do something. When it comes to a life, a person shouldn't leave rooms for regrets, if they can help it. Be it their own, or anyone else's... I have my fair share of regrets as far as that goes and didn't want any more.

I studied the scene one last time—I didn't see any debris that might indicate an accident, but that might be why the hatch was open and all their things were thrown out on the road.

That settled it.

I took a flashlight out of my purse, well, a penlight. It's bright—for the first time it didn't seem bright enough.

When I was getting out, I was torn between locking up—which I'd always do if I couldn't keep the car in sight—and leaving the doors unlocked and maybe even the driver's door open a little.

Ultimately, I decided to lock all the doors and keep the car running. I would keep my remote entry key in my hand.
Then I got out.

I dialed 9-1-1 again and closed the door with my freehand. I pressed the lock button on the remote. Inside the speakers throbbed—I didn't realize I was listening to the music so loud.

At the time, it really bothered me that I couldn't tell what song was playing, but I knew the rhythm. No - I just remembered. It was *The Red*, by Chevelle.

I love human memory's queue.

The night air felt great, but that was the only good thing about being out there.

I'm sure there are plenty of people who've never smelled anything dead, much less a dead person, unless it was at a funeral—though an embalmed person smells a lot different than someone who's just dead—and rotting. And dead people smell different from other dead things.

I was pretty little when I found out what death smells like, mostly from animals hit on the road. I learned the difference between the smell of road kill and that of human decay by the time I was a teenager.

They say once you know, you never forget it.

You *never* forget it.

So I knew it wasn't that these people hit a deer and hiked away from their accident—I knew I wasn't going to like what I saw.

No bars on the phone.
I reached out for the end of the gate.

I was about to swing it closed when something cut through the light behind me. I turned to it—her, I guess, because I could see the shape of a skirt in the silhouette. Her steps were soggy. She must have been in the ditch.

I asked if she was okay. A high, thrilled kind of whine squeezed out of her throat. It sounded relieved. It kind of sounded like someone with emphysema airily delighting in a surprise.

I asked again.

Then something grabbed my foot. I instinctively yanked it back and my foot came free.
I looked down just in time to see a small hand recoil under the open station wagon gate. The feel of where the little fingers gripped me made my scalp prickle. I was startled. The last thing I expected was to see that thing, like a chubby, hairless tarantula, clutching my shoe.

Then, I felt bad about how I jerked my foot away. I thought I might have hurt or scared them.

I gave the door a shove to close it.

There was a child there—no more than nine.

I'm guessing he was naturally that skinny, but he seemed too tiny to me. Like a board. With a head.
He reached out again.

I stepped around him so I was at his side. That's when I noticed the blood. He was hurt really bad. His side looked like he'd slid on a giant kitchen grater. He couldn't talk.

By my left foot was a brown, paisley printed faux leather purse. All its contents were scattered around my feet. I was sorry for stepping on, what I assumed, were the woman's belongings.

I lay my left hand between the small boy's shoulders to calm him. He was frantic.

I dialed 9-1-1 again.

I asked the woman if this was her son—she'd come within arm's reach and covered me in her shadow. The boy was struggling weakly.

I was about to tell him he should lay still, when she lunged at me.

I stumbled back, only because she was in my personal space. The boy was making sounds like a pissed off cat. Roww Roww Roww –over other garbled sounds.

I said "hey" or something, when she reached for me again. Her arms didn't drop. They just kept reaching.

I backed up enough, while on ground level, that I could stand without being right in her bleeding face.

"I said—are you okay?" I said. I heard alarm in my voice. I needed to get back to the kid.

I went around the other side of the car. She started to come over it.

Crawling across the hood, through the light from my headlights, I saw blood in her hair and on her flailing legs. And on the scrambling hands, that looked like big bloody spiders tap dancing on the car hood. She'd got most of the way on top before she started to slide back.

"Watch out for the kid!" I yelled. "Sweet Jesus!"

I thought I'd hear her feet land softly—land softly on the kid. I was relieved when I heard them touch the road.

I circled around to the back of the station wagon again. With the gate closed I could easily see the boy, but he'd pulled himself under the car and was starting to come out again, very slowly. The woman just stood there—like when I first saw her. I dialed 9-1-1 again. I heard the computer.

"Are you okay?" I said firmly.
I asked her what happened. I demanded to know.
She kept wheezing and started out into the light. Her eyes were wrong. Really wrong. The boy was emerging from under the rear license plate. His eyes were wrong too.
I can't describe it.
I probably don't have to, unless this was found well after this is over.
...if it's ever over.
But I can't describe it anyway so it doesn't matter.

I'm not happy about what I did next, but I'm going to tell you. I got back in my car and locked the doors. I dropped the remote in the cup holder, behind my soft serve cup. I pressed on the brake and put the car in reverse when she slammed her face into the window beside me. She broke several of her front teeth out and kept chomping against the glass. Her tongue was free to flop, where the teeth had been. Even while chomping, she was licking. Her bloody, spider hands slapped the frame between the driver's side window and the windshield. I heard her pull on the door handle.

I looked over my shoulder and stomped on the gas. My neck felt so vulnerable—I imagined her breaking through the glass with her face.

I imagined a mouth, much bigger than hers, clamping on my neck.

I imagined the wound and the texture of my neck meat like that of a giant celery stick. All sinew and tissue.

I didn't imagine blood. Just the feel of the bite.

All teeth and gums and flopping tongue.

I braked hard and threw it into drive as soon as I had room to do a U-turn. My headlights ran across the two of them. She was running at me. She looked like a puppet, something gangly, with string joints and utterly strengthless in herself, being manipulated by unskilled hands.

I was making my way back to where the state trooper pulled me over. I saw headlights in front of me and soon I saw the police car in the approach between the road and the everlasting South Dakota plains.

I drove past the squad car, did a U-turn again, and pulled onto the shoulder. I turned on my interior lights and got out. I didn't want to walk up to his car, so I waved at him with both arms.

The International Distress Signal, as we were taught in *Open Water*.

The officer got out. This time I saw his partner, who looked "no bullshit" for sure.

Before he could say anything I yelled that I needed help. His partner must have heard because jumped out. They both did a strange thing. They drew their guns.

I assume that's a strange thing to do to someone who just called for help.

"Bit?"
I think I started to say, "What?"
"Are you *bit*?" the "easy speaking" officer yelled.

I thought I heard him wrong so I took the opportunity to talk.
My heart was racing. My blood pressure was making my ears
ring—I felt a cold heavy pressure behind my ears. My upper
arms were tingling. I felt ice water in my veins. I felt needles in
my chest—the contrast in my vision was getting intense—his
gun leveled with my head.

"There's a woman and child up that route you gave me. They
must have been in an a—"

He yelled the question again—moving the gun with emphasis
on each word.

"*Bit*? No-not bit. I couldn't get through to 9-1-1 so I didn't
know what to do. The lady is moving around all right, but I'm
worried about the boy," I explained. My arms flopped heavily
against my sides in something like a shrug. Did he hear me?

He held a flashlight up over his gun and it seemed like forever
until he said anything.

"Are you hurt?" he asked.
I told him, "No."

"They need help. I don't know what happened to them—but
they're hurt," I added.
The gun and flashlight lowered. He looked like he was seeing
me for the first time.

The car was in the middle of the road, I told him.
He turned to the radio on his shoulder and called something in.

"Do you *need* to get to Wisconsin?"
I stared at him dumbly for a moment. *Need* to?
"I'm heading home."

His shoulders drooped and if he sighed it was too quiet for me to hear, but it was a "sigh" movement.

He told me to go back that way and to drive around the car. He told me not to stop, that someone was on the way.

"I feel bad for leaving them. And I'm worried about the little boy. His mom was acting really weird."

Someone will take care of them, he said. The words were right, but the tone was wrong. I didn't know if I could just drive by.

Okay—the lady freaked the hell out of me. She was obviously hysterical or something. Maybe completely fucking mental—but that fragile looking little boy—that bleeding, hurting, desperate little kid?

I was driving a lot slower when I came upon the luggage again. In the same moment, the arch of the headlights lit the station wagon. The gate was slightly ajar. Woman and child were nowhere in sight. I wondered if someone else hadn't come along. A few different country roads came out on the stretch behind me…

I cringe whenever I feel tires run over frogs on the road—I cringed the same way when I felt those people's things thump-thump under the wheels.

I never saw the two again or any reason for the car to have been left in the middle of the road. To be honest, I didn't look too deeply into it.

I followed the officer's route back to I90-E.

Back on the interstate, I passed several vehicles on the shoulder. Most were packed like sardines.

I moved to the opposite side of the road to avoid a car straddling the shoulder and lane. There were several people gathered by it. Too many to have all been passengers.

I think I would have stopped if it had been a family stuck out there in the middle of the night, but they were all adults.

And they looked like they were looting it.

I went by slow. I tried to see what was going on.

The group looked up in unison—their faces blank and full of energy at the same time.
Potential energy.
I felt threatened.

I'd interrupted them, obviously, doing something wrong, probably illegal, at about 2:30 in the morning.

Their looks said, "Should we get her too?"

My car was dark—they stood in the strong, warm beams of my headlights. They shouldn't have been able to see much more than the light, but I felt like they saw me anyway—in the dark, with my lights in their eyes. They looked straight into my eyes. Maybe deeper.

They could have been responsible for what I came across on the detour...

I called 9-1-1 again, repeating the license plate so I wouldn't forget it. The same message again and again. Then I gave up.

What the hell is going on around here, I thought.

I pulled the audio cord out of my dash and turned on the radio. I got static, but I wasn't surprised—I was now four hours away from the radio station Carrie had tuned in back in Hill City. I pressed scan. It ran in circles like a gerbil and then stopped. There was a blip of sound, then nothing. I was going to press scan again, but decided not to. In my gut, I knew there wasn't anything there. I put the audio cable back in. The speakers filled with soothing music, starting somewhere in the first half of *Darkness* by Disturbed. I felt the knots start to loosen through my muscles and was submitting to the music.
I screamed when my phone rang.

It was Marie again.
I answered. She was there.
"Are you okay," I asked.
"How far are you?"

I told her I was about an hour from Sioux Falls.
Then she asked me if I was okay.
What a night I'd had!

Ordinarily I would have been thrilled to tell the story of such crazy happenings—if only I wasn't afraid that the person I was about to tell might have similar or worse experiences to relate. Fear squeezed my heart—*where are the girls?*

I said I was fine.

I said my radio wasn't getting stations. As if that summed it up.

She said her husband, Patrick, told her he'd heard people weren't operating them or they were being forced off the air.

I thought of one of my favorite actresses, Kathy Bates' character in Stephen King's *The Stand* movie/miniseries— when she gets shot down by soldiers when she tries to stay on the air and keep people informed.

What exactly didn't they want people to hear that most folks didn't already know?

I've since thought about *The Stand* a lot.

"What's going on?" I felt stupid to ask.
She didn't know.
So before she answered, I added that I felt like we'd slipped into some alternate reality.

She told me she thought all drunks were on the lamb:
"Lushcanthropy"
I laughed.
I asked what else Patrick said.
She answered with a question.

How much had I seen?

Her tone, stiff and dreadful, like a crime boss whose best friend has just accidently witnessed him murder a whole family. I'd never heard her voice sound like that. *Never.* A weight filled my stomach like I'd chugged a gallon of concrete.

I went blank. I didn't really know what I saw.
Then the phone starting cutting out—so she started talking about that. She started talking faster. Said something about avoiding towns.

I thought about Dee, waiting for her flight. Was she at the airport? Had she got a hotel room? Rapid City isn't tiny…

Then I heard Marie say that I should get gas even if I didn't need it—if it looked safe. She said she had less than a quarter of a tank. That she'd tried twice, but got too scared to stay and wait.

My thoughts flew to the looters—to the bloody mouth chomping on my window.

Then I lost her signal.
"Damn," I said.

If I'd had her on the line *now* and been cut off, that curse wouldn't have just laid there flat—like I dropped it. I would have been frantic. Nothing was desperate yet. No amount of fear was what the situation deserved.

I pulled over.
When I put the car in park, all the doors automatically unlocked. I quickly pushed the lock button and tried to call everyone I could think of, even though it was late.

I thought I had a good enough reason, by then, to justify a calling anyone at that ungodly hour. At this point, there was nothing too sacred, I wouldn't dare interrupt it.
In the end, the phone never rang anywhere.
No bars. No shirt. No service.

So I pulled back out on the road.

There was a gas station up ahead. I didn't need any—obviously. I drive a small car—not a hummer. But Marie didn't say it for laughs. Which wasn't like her at all.

She was always the funny one in our group. At least, she always made me laugh—to the point where we'd all be clutching our aching sides and warning how close we were to pissing ourselves—not idle threats either.

The gas station was closed. Most would be at this hour, but Pay-At-The-Pump is a night traveler's friend.

There were a lot of night travelers.

Lycanthropy? Vampires?
A lot of campers.
A lot of people away from home, enjoying the summer, blissfully unaware that a fiber of normalcy was loose.
We were the exception.

Few people go a day without checking their email or FB, but maybe people who live online aren't the ones that go camping. I don't know.

But all of us had cell phones we weren't answering or had shut off. In hindsight, from people's faces—they knew a lot more than I did.
I decided not to stop.
I decided something else.
No more cities.

Once I got into Minnesota, I'd know more roads. I'd skirt every city I could. There were plenty of "out-in-the-boondocks" gas stations with Pay-At-The-Pump. Why mess with the gas station version of Black Friday? You'd have thought gas had gone below three bucks.

I'm gonna have to call it a day, it's getting late.

I haven't really been paying attention. So....

No more long stories short.

Oct 25 6:42am

Spitting snow today. I'm getting things in order. I plan to walk into town today and find a muzzle for Mr. Ages. I plan to be gone no more than ten hours.

It puts everything into perspective, how far can I go within a given amount of time? How far will I have to go to escape a winter I can't survive?

7:03am

I have to leave Mr. Ages inside because I'd be too afraid he'd follow me… and if he didn't, I'd lose my mind worrying about him.

But if I lock him inside and something happens to me I'd be sentencing him to death. A horrible and drawn out death.

I'm afraid of what he'd do worrying about me.

He has separation anxiety... I think I might too.

7:10am

There's only one thing to do—I am going to get my car.

5:50pm

I was telling you how all this began... Where was I?

It was almost 10am when I got back from Hill City. I stopped at my mailbox. My skin was cold. I was still shaking. Disturbed, unnerved, not dealing… like I'd just had an accident… a brush with death. I pawed at the tin tombstone shaped mouth and yanked down on the claw shaped knob. I felt in the empty space, not trusting or maybe not understanding the shadowy nothing I found inside.

I asked for a mail hold. Deliveries were scheduled to resume the next day, but there were newspapers in the open-faced bin on the left.

I pushed the only button, on the remote clipped to the visor, and watched the garage door start creeping up its track.

My driveway wouldn't have been very long if it didn't have a wide curve in it. Aesthetics, I guess. Maybe something to do with the intricate system of streams running like lace from greater bodies of water nearby…

A wimpy tree, about 4 feet tall, stands in the enclosed, grassy center of the curve. My plum tree.

The garage door was nearly open when I reached it. I only had to wait a second. The garage is attached to the house. I took my purse and newspapers in one hand, had my house keys ready in the other, before I got out of the car. I locked it behind me. I'd get my luggage later.

I didn't have to look to unlock the front door. I only clinked outside the lock twice before the key went in—my eyes were busy with the newspapers.
I stepped over a FedEx box as I entered.

I locked the door and deadbolt and put the keys in my jeans' pocket. I never do that. Countertop, by the microwave, every time. *Every* time. Maybe once in every four months would I set them somewhere else.

I don't pocket them.

I turned on the TV to try to catch the news. No signal. I was dialing home—the other "home"—where parents live.

The answering machine picked up. I hate that the message says they're not home. I had urged my mom not to say things like that because you never know who's calling.

At the beep, I almost wailed, "Where are you?!?"

"Hi mom or dad. I'm home early," not that they knew about the vacation. "Call me as soon as you get this."

Then I said "please" in a voice I hardly recognized. It was throaty and I felt my nerves failing. My mind was reeling. If I cried, I didn't know if I could stop. I needed to keep my shit together.

My thoughts were then, the same as now.

What's going on?

Is everyone okay?

When you know who "everyone" implies—you just feel each name. The word is made of each name.

I don't know why, but I called my job.

I got the answering service.

Closed at 10am on a Friday?

I dialed again. Same.

I've decided I did this is because my boss is such an asshole. He would jump on any excuse to give me hell. I don't suck his cock, but I know as a fact others do/did. His dirty jokes and the weird sexual commentary of my co-workers or customers creeped me out. When I let him know it bothered me—then I was suddenly a troublemaker. I wasn't part of the "team".

To hell with him, I thought. Then I pictured the things that filled my mind when I thought of the people I love and imagined the worst case scenarios… and wished no less for him and, to be honest, much, much worse.

Then I started dialing every person I could think of, again, while spreading out the newspapers in order. It should have been eight days of papers. I only had four, but someone could have taken them.

Chronologically the headlines and other front page articles were reading like this—oldest to newest:

THE SICK CONGEST LOCAL HOSPITALS
ER Doc Bit by Pulseless Patient
Sheriff's Department Urges Extra Precautions from Home Invaders

CDC ISSUES HIGHEST ALERT
Nat'l Guard and Police Coop to Control Violence
Missouri Doctor Finds "Fever" in Primates

AIRPORTS AND GOVERNMENT OFFICES CLOSE
Hospital Leaks: Number of Reported Deaths - Tip of the Iceberg
Doctors Say, "Fever cause of hallucinations and hysteria"

GOVERNOR TEMPLE: "We have it under control."
Doctors Now Say: "New Strain of Rabies"
Government Facilities to Reopen

How many people were dead by that time?

...Is *this* the way the world ends? Not with a whimper, but a scream?

I mouthed "Christ" and tried to absorb words that were blurring.

On the phone, dialing the first number, I heard the end of a message, "...as dialed. Please check your number and dial again."
The next, "...no longer in service..."
The phone rattled against my ear.

The edges of the newspaper made fluttering sounds in the tips of my fingers.
The ugly tone to each number pressed.
The terrible silence.
Did they make it home?

My eyes were burning.
I looked up from the papers.
I let them go and carried the phone to the kitchen window.

I opened the one over the sink, too high for anyone outside of the NBA to reach without a ladder.
I could faintly hear the tornado sirens in town.

Out of the corner of my left eye, I saw someone cutting across my yard. I could tell he noticed the distant siren too.
I knocked the metal stopper in the sink when I moved to see him better.

He tried to see me better too.
When he turned—half his face was gone.

The left side of his body was soaked in blood. I couldn't or wouldn't register what he was holding in that hand.
He started for the house.

I'd left the front garage door unlocked for a parcel, the FedEx that I was expecting to arrive while I was gone.

It was still unlocked.

Suddenly, the front door seemed a long ways away.

I ran, driving my hip angrily against a chair. It clattered loudly when it turned over. The pounding of my foot falls were the only other thing in my ears.

I threw open the locks and reached the garage door just as he did. Eight inches away, he stared into my eyes. I flipped the lock and ran to the rear garage door. It was already locked. I had to be sure.

The man was trying the knob.
He clawed at the glass.
His eyes bugged out as he fought with the knob that wouldn't turn. Then blood started running from them—his eyes were popping out.
I locked the screen door and locked myself inside.

I don't remember a lot of what happened next. I realized it was later in the day; the sun was on the other side of the house. The underside of my right wrist was pressed into my right eye and my elbow felt like it had pierced my knee. I was sitting by the door.

My body felt settled into the position, like I was clay and almost hardened. I had little will to move.

My right eye ached and had a hard time focusing, after having pressure on it so long. My face was wet and sticky with drying tears. I wasn't crying anymore. I just needed a tissue.
I got up and was wobbly.

My ass had no circulation and felt like I had a golf ball in my butt crack.

I stood there stiffly, both desperate to begin making sense of things and planning while also trying hard not to think at all for a second.

Then I heard scratching outside.

I went to the open kitchen window and saw lots of them (what seemed like "lots" at the time)—four—busy bodies trying to get to me.
Only then did it occur to me that I'd blacked out or something—what if they had gotten in? What if they got in right then?

I wasn't sure what would happen then. I knew what happened in the movies. I knew I would die.
Or I was pretty sure.

But I didn't even know if they <u>were </u>dead or if they were demented or something. The newspaper said something about rabies—they were fresher back then, remember, than most of them are now. They pretty much looked and smelled like living people… only some of them were hurt in ways I don't think someone could survive for long, if at all.

At the moment it was as simple as this:
I didn't want them near me.

I closed the window and locked it. I dropped the blinds. Even clenched to the lip of the sink, my hands were vibrating.

Was anybody's first thought, "*HEY*! The zombies! *Finally*. We knew you'd show up." Or did most people just make excuses and believe what they read in the paper.

-

On the way back to Rhinelander, I had people run at my car. I saw folks wandering too. In the dark, they were gray and obscure shapes. Strange black blobs on the road, on the shoulder...

I only saw-saw them at dawn—the red light coated everything like candied apples. The world looked like Hell.

red sun in morning, sailors take warning

It was surreal, the precipice of morning—all that red light against pure black shadows.
I saw them going after people.
I saw what happened.
I remember, sitting a stoplight, and a small, terrified voice inside me reluctantly suggesting that these people were undead.

The representative voices of every other part of my being snarled at it to shut up... still silencing the voice did nothing against my sight. A selfish parent running far ahead of the child, whose scream was so shrill, if it cried "mother" or "father", I could not tell. Even if the parent thought to go back, it was too late, their black shape was devoured by other black shapes. I pushed my thumb into the release of my seatbelt, keeping my eyes locked on the charging toddler, without thinking, without putting the car in park, half jumped out the door—when the deep inky shadows of the ditch separating parent from child, consumed the little human—I lost sight of her... On the further bank, in the morning light, forms of pure red poured down toward it and those of pure black silhouette...coming after.

Otep's version of *Not to Touch the Earth* was just beginning, while I idled at a stoplight, watching the end of the world through the filter of a sanguine sunrise... I always thought that song was destined to be in a zombie movie. For the first time I didn't like it for that. It was scaring the shit out of me or, at least, not helping. The pounding of my heart was lost in the pounding of drums and bass. I didn't know which was louder in my ears. My left leg, poised, mid-leap, recoiled into the relative safety of the vehicle. I pulled the door shut slowly. It clicked, though not fully flush with the frame.

A DOOR IS AJAR
<bing> <bing> <bing>

My mouth was dry, agape with fear and disbelief. I listened to the motor running. I looked across the chaos, which seemed oblivious of me...

And I said fuck it to the red light—that hadn't changed in minutes—pressed hard on the accelerator and got the hell out of there.

There were plenty of witnesses, but I wasn't afraid of anyone talking... I shoved that little voice somewhere deeper than my gut, into the shit where everything you block out is drowned. Only by the time I reached home, struggling to do so much as check the mail, the truth was refusing to be ignored... for fear,

I think, of what it would cost me to continue denying it.

-

About how I lost my car in the first place...

I only lasted a month at my own house, on my supplies, before I tried to go out. What I thought was essential a month and a week or so before, which didn't include any edibles, was still in my trunk. I had been too afraid to go into the garage.

That was going to have to change.

Just in case, I found the shoebox where I kept all my photos and chose my favorites of each person I love. I got my spare glasses, my supply of contacts, first aid supplies, my small external hard drive with a backup of everything on my computer, an LED lantern, took the cell phone and MP3 chargers, wallet, and a few personal things out of my purse and put on extra layers of clothes (including my Zombie Apocalypse t-shirt) and then I grabbed a few other things I thought I should have on me at all times.

I considered my collection of books. It was hard to imagine leaving any of them behind—all but a few of my favorites, those I thought I knew by heart. My Victorian Poetry collection is littered with post-its. My copy of *NIMH* is little more than ribbons anymore. There's a lot of Michael Crichton. Stephen King. Phillip Pullman. Richard Matheson. Harold Schechter and Nathaniel Philbrick—thanks to Dee.

I don't know how many people would agree with who I think are history's most important authors.

At the forefront of my list would be A.A. Milne, who wrote *Winnie-the-Pooh*. There are a lot of important truths and life/philosophical lessons in them that I think are ignored or don't get the credit they deserve because they aren't delivered to us in big words and as books for "adults".

Plato and Lovecraft would be in my top ten too.

This is impossible...

I could go on forever if I went into it.

I'm not going to.

Of the authors I adore, Cormac McCarthy would be the only one to contribute to the load of items to keep on me at all times. I actually have two copies of the single title I chose. *The Road*. One, a first edition, is flimsy and tattered. The second copy, which stayed at my house to hopefully serve another reader, features a picture from the movie.

After seeing the movie, I always picture "the man" as Viggo Mortenson. I can't remember what I imagined before that.

The others I considered most seriously were *NIMH* and *Pooh*. Both I'm sure I know by heart.

I couldn't leave *The Road* behind. Since the first time I read it, I found comfort in it. I expected to have to look for it there again.

I needed to see if I could find a store that was open.

What would I do if there weren't any, I thought. I didn't really think they would be open, but I wasn't ready to start breaking into places either.

I took a hammer and a flat head screwdriver—one that always struck me as being particularly long. I wore my dark-gray pea coat. It goes down almost to my knees. Probably no one could tell I was "armed". I still think that's a good thing.

I tried to psyche myself up.
I nervously thought: I'd do whatever I had to.
Then I locked up my house, got in my car and drove about four miles—with busy bodies following.
That was when I met "The Mob". Neighborhood Watch, I also call them. The cluster of dead that hang together, hunt together, wander together.
Turtle was one of them.

The ones who ate the woman that lived kitty corner from me.

I slowed down instinctively—it wasn't in my system to run people down and I hadn't yet "killed" any of them. It's not as easy as they make it look in the movies. It's hard to unlearn such things as being wary of hurting others, of speeding, of legal consequences. How moral consequences might change…

When my car shuddered and died, I immediately regretted not stepping on the gas instead.

I only knew what was in the books and movies—that might come down to knowing nothing. Wouldn't one be up shit creek if dragons showed up and we had to sort through all of fiction's ways to kill them? More closely related to zombies popping up everywhere—what would I do against vampires or werewolves?

I'd just have to take what I "know" and pray.
So that's exactly what I did.

I giggled, despite my fear or maybe because of it, when I imagined *Night of the Living Dead* being used as an instructional video in schools of the future. Living Dead 101: "Pay attention to their mistakes."
"Make note of the good use of unlikely tools for putting down the dead. And I don't mean insults. Ha. Ha."
It's easy to imagine the tests.

The dead pressed on all sides of the car. I sat and thought a long time about the mess I was in before I decided how I was going to get out of it. In retrospect, stupidly, I did not consider trying to start it again.

I put on my bag and prayed earnestly.
I lowered the seats as flat as possible, so I had as much room as possible for moving around. I crawled to the rear passenger side door. I put my hands to the glass and slapped on it.

Half of them moved to be nearer to me. That was probably enough. The ones that were stubborn stayed in the same places where they first fixed their eyes on me, refusing to give up their spot and tried to get in where they were.
I thought briefly about crawling into the trunk and seeing if they'd lose interest. I'm claustrophobic and the suggestion made me sick.

I'd thought about going through the roof—a really dumb idea. Once I decided what I was going to do, I just hoped they were dumb and I could distract them like animals.

I reached forward and rolled down the passenger window—just enough for them to get their fingers through. That got a few of the stubborn ones interested. Maybe they could more easily smell me.

As quick as I could, I pulled my keys and kicked open the driver's side door. It hit several of them, but still others had been at the passenger door behind me.

I felt them grab me, but they didn't get good holds. Not until one bitch caught my hair—I broke her hand off at the wrist with one frantic swing of the hammer—this didn't register until hours later—and I ran. I ran into the first yard I came to. The front door was locked. I ran down to the basement's walkout and saw several busy bodies inside.

I ran to the next yard and a zombie intercepted me. It grabbed a handful of my bag. I slipped out of it, but kept a hold on one of the arm straps. I put all my weight into swinging the bag and unbalancing him. I went down too, but he let go long enough for me to get the bag back. I held it by the top handle and crawled until I got my feet under me, stooped, and moved hunched until I was running.

Evolution Chart of a Zombie Apocalypse Survivor?

In my peripheral vision I saw them coming.

My eyes were jumping. They kept finding more of them.
I ran past a van where people must have been taken off guard trying to leave. There was a zombie in the open back—eating a face, like it was eating corn on the cob.

The edge of the yard sloped downward. There I tripped and I spilled into reeds and water. I choked on a mouthful. I gasped and, coughing and gagging, I pushed through the wall of waxy, squeaking, man tall reeds. When they opened up, I was rib deep in the creek. The current wasn't strong, but I was tired and its push felt like a bulldozer. It carried me about ten feet by the time I clawed my way to the reeds on the other side and pulled myself into them.

The yard went up somewhat steeply along the water, just like on the other side.

I ran to the house—a gray two-story with a three stall detached garage. There was an SUV tucked into the opposite side of the yard, where the creek wraps around the property. Its hood, divided by an oak tree.

I ran past two bags and a mostly eaten corpse when I came upon the body of a man sprawled out on the sidewalk that surrounded the flower beds. In one outstretched hand he clenched a set of keys.

I kicked the body. It didn't move. I stooped to grab the keys and saw motion that was too fucking close for comfort. It was the Postman—that bulbous headed freak that, even dead, seemed like his lips were redder than they should be. So saggy—like the upside down hemorrhoid covered asshole of a chicken, but pumped up with collagen.
I'm not making this shit up.
I know it's weird, but I know what a chicken's asshole looks like—and I know what the Postman's mouth looks like—the rest are the missing details.

His eyes didn't look entirely blank. I think I project something there. Remember, I think he's a creep. So nothing, not even the way he might have washed clothes or wrapped a present, when he was alive, would be free of seeming "off" to me.

He struck me as a pervert, a creep, a weirdo, a Peeping Tom, panty sniffing sheep-raper.

Since the day I moved to that street, he made my skin crawl.
I don't think people should be judged on how they look, but
sometimes there's something to instinct too.
No arguing that he is a creep now.
Then, he was coming up the driveway, and fast.
I yanked the keys free.
The rest was a blur.

I remember getting inside, slamming the door, locking it and
shaking fear off for about an hour. After, I hollered around,
ready to deal with anything. I wanted whatever or whoever
might be inside to know I was there.

Come and get it—get it over with.

When I'd stood there as long as I could stand and I heard
nothing and nobody showed up, I went looking for a place to
rest a little. I found a made bed, in what I assumed was a guest
room, because there were no personal affects. I flopped down,
face first, exhausted.

It was dark when I woke up to creaking floors—to be exact, the
bedroom's creaking floor. It was carpet, so all other movement
was muffled.

There was congested groaning or moaning or whatever the
fuck sounds these things make—they strike me as accordions
or bag pipes. They're not breathing, there's just air in there,
making horrible, hellish, ungodly sounds.

Something blocked out the lower half of the doorway, like a
black igloo.

Like Dr. Seuss's Grinch, I slid off the bed, on my stomach, to my knees, to my hands and then belly again as something grabbed at the covers on the other side.

I heard a sound like a hundred shoes in a sack hitting the ground as the thing, on hands and knees, collapsed—

JENGA!

—onto the floor on the opposite side of the—thank God— *heavy* wooden queen sized bed. I could vaguely tell what it was doing. Of course, it was worming its way under, but it couldn't even get its shoulders under. If it wedged hard enough, I thought it might be able to lift the bed. It was pushing hard.

Since then, I have seen rotting ones that have literally crawled out of themselves to get where they want to go.

I backed up—my heartbeat was deafening.
I vaguely remember finding the lamp, but I *do* remember how it felt in my hand. I held it just under the bulb.

At some point I tossed aside the shade.
I yanked the cord free when I reached the end of *its* reach.

The busy body was trying to get out. I planted my right foot on the corner of the bed and gave it a hard shove. The grunt of effort was high—wanting to be a scream. Some of the undead's heavy round shoulder meat sloughed off like cheese on a mandolin.

The bed moved farther than I thought it would.
Then I was clubbing it.

I clubbed it until its head was gone. I stood over it, lamp raised, fearful it wasn't over. Terrified that, like some video game bosses, that once one "version" was destroyed, it would become something more horrible.

Only when I was satisfied it was dead and gone, I took my flashlight and I scoured the house from top to bottom.

On the way back to the bedroom I realized why it hadn't attacked me when I got there. It definitely heard me—it was just so big that it took that long to reach me.

It drug itself to the room like an army man. I could see where it pulled itself up the bedroom door frame. I followed the red-brown hand prints, like animal tracks, as its hands and belly were slowly defleshed from drawing and dragging such a heavy burden. I followed it to the basement where I found a busy body that was already dispatched.

I blamed the one in the basement for "turning" the big one upstairs. It must have felt awful to survive the encounter only to have suffered a bite anyway.

I dumped the basement zombie out of an upstairs window. I had to get out onto the roof to shove it over the side.

I couldn't move the bedroom intruder, but I couldn't stand him being there—even if I barricaded the door—and I wasn't going out to try and find another place.

I didn't want to go out ever again.

Until now.

And even now, I'm not going because I want to.

No more reminiscing...

I need my car.

Oct 26 7:05am

Made it to the edge of the yard.

Couldn't make myself go farther.

1:49pm

I was thinking….life expectancy can't be based on age anymore, but on average survival time.

It has been 142 days.

When I am brave, I am a strange thing. Adventurer… Empress… I may be the sole inheritor of the earth. I'm helpless but to go and let what good there is, out in it, serve me.

When I am a coward, I am a frustrating, procrastinating creature. I am rat-like, tentative, wise enough to be wary of everything—to see everything as an obstacle or opportunity. Fearful, because it is safe to be fearful… all the while, having a feeling that I better understand this world, and am thereby more powerful, than the part of me who feels like sole inheritor of it. When you are alone, you cannot survive operating like one person. I have to be everyone I need.

Do I stay here because I know this place by heart? Why does that almost worthless comfort ground me here when starvation and freezing to death are the alternative?

…because I am not freezing or starving yet…

Oct 27 11:13am

How long did you want to live? Would you want to live
forever?

Do you?
What are *you* living for?
I've got me and my dog.
It could be worse.
I could be alone.
So hell yeah he's worth it.

I wouldn't want to live *forever*.

But I'm not going to die today.

Oct 28 5:33pm

Lucius Seneca suggested, "As long as you live, keep learning
how to live."

The busy body that tried to get me from under the bed was too
big for me to move with anything but God's help.

I had to cut him up to move him out. I don't want to write or
think about what that was like. I couldn't live with him in here.
Could you? I don't pretend to know everything about them.
What if suddenly two deaths weren't enough to kill them?

God help me. I'm not sorry. I ~~did~~ *will* do what I have to, to
live.

I'm not going to roll over and die.

When/if this is ever over, no one is going to say I'm ungrateful for even one breath.

6:02pm

Mr. Ages is beside me. The A/C is tossing his coat.

I can tell that he knows something is beginning—a new chapter in this journey—what is about to become a Journey. I touch the softness of his fur and wonder when will be the next time that I will have a chance to wash him. What state am I leading us to? Would we have been okay where we were? If not, am I leading us to worse? He trusts me, but he's also wondering, "What next?" So am I.

There are a few miles behind us. We're at an intersection. There's dead here—there is a lot of junk. A lot of discarded belongings, people didn't plan on abandoning or they would have left them in their homes. These are things that mattered.

Many Americans have ancestors who had to make similarly hard choices to those of these modern pioneers. I pity them. I pity the heartbreak of the child who was told they may only bring one toy. I pity the collector and the person whose heart is almost physically attached to an heirloom too large or heavy to retain. We invest ourselves in obtaining them. Our sentiments in retaining them. I think it's okay to grieve things…

I pity the diabetic, the asthmatic, the arthritic, all the other folks who might be surviving just fine, were they not dependent on medicine to make life bearable or possible. To say nothing of the invalids, the elderly… blind and deaf people… anyone dependent on wheelchairs or walkers.

I need to start appreciating my situation and the advantages I've always had.

Who the fuck am I to still be here?

What happens now?
I feel like shit. I feel a queer kind of excitement mingling with paralyzing terror. I'm apprehensive. Anxious.

I meet my own eyes in the mirror behind the visor. They are bloodshot and small dark boomerangs are developing under my red-rimmed eyes. I sweep a swatch of light brown hair behind my ear so I can see most of my face. I wish I looked more determined. Braver.

I'm still shaken up from retrieving the car. I smell the fluids from the busy bodies I dealt with on the bottoms of my shoes.

My lower and upper lip mirror each other. I always thought something about their shape always made me look like I had my mind made up, when in fact I rarely did.

There is always room for doubt.

About ten years ago I did something almost exactly like this— when I ran away from home. I was afraid and, just like now, the only certainty was that there was no certainty. Just like now, I didn't feel like staying was an option.

I'm idling on a broad plain of lanes where only 145 days ago, cars would have filled the space like a herd of cattle pushing down their designated lanes. There are signs for going to Madison, Milwaukee and Chicago...

Someone took the time to hang a foam poster board over part of the sign to Chicago that says:

CHICAGO IS DEAD

I stare at this for some time.

I already know that even small towns are out of the question, but it's good to be warned when I'm getting close to someplace really big.

Every way is as good as the next.

Mr. Ages thinks so too.

I am living, not surviving.

A lot of billboards have been covered with signs about places for survivors to go. The signs call them "Disaster Relief Stations". In this situation, I wouldn't relinquish control of my life to the government. The people running them are no different than the rest of us—scared and willing to do anything to stay safe, with little or no consideration for other people.

How many people completely abandoned their jobs to get back to their families as fast as they could, no matter how important their duties were to the majority?

How could anyone blame them?

There will be people on power trips—there always are. With no higher authority to report to if someone abuses that power…

No thank you.

These stations are run by people. Just people.
People are selfish.

People will favor some people more than others. They have a hard time being objective.

A lot of times people get put in positions because of their connections, not qualifications. People can be really stupid. Power corrupts. And people are the kind of animals that, when running to get or get away, trample other people to death. Shit—people trample other people to death for game consoles.

I chose to head toward Chicago. But I'll be swinging wide.

I'm playing my MP3 player so I don't hear the dead saying nothing on the radio. Instead I'm hearing Anneke Van Giersbergen's *Drive*.

I'm singing along, hard and loud.

Is there any other way when you listen to that song?

I roll down the window a little and something like fresh air streams in through space. Something like the way air was… Mr. Ages stands on my lap to sniff at it. His feet dig into my thigh meat. I shoulder him away and roll down his window a little.

I hear myself laugh and it makes me want to cry.

The sun is setting and the world, again, looks beautiful to me. Even the chaos that collapsed on us is beautiful if you can imagine it worse.

I can.

I've already imagined worse for everyone and everything. Trust me, we need to not think that—about any of that.

You're breathing.

Maybe that's as good as it gets, but I need to tell you, that's enough to live on.

Maybe I can say that because I haven't been hurt like maybe you have.

I don't want to compare scars.

I'm just coping.

So I'm going to go for now—forward, ever forward—and tonight I'm wishing all of us—ALL of us, the best.

Oct 29 9:24am

I LOVE MUSIC.

Maybe I'm getting old, but I don't often find bands anymore that I like—I like just what I like. What I liked. So I feel really blessed to have got my hands on a couple gems before the mine caved it, sort of speak. I picked up these two cd's just before the reunion with my friends:

Imagine Dragons—I bought *Night Visions* just because I like dragons and I had a gift card I hadn't gotten around to using. Not great reasons. I didn't realize that I'd heard some of their songs before, because the radio station I listened to most of the time rarely bothered to say who was responsible for the music they played.

The other was The Neighbourhood's *I Love You.* I bought it for *Sweater Weather,* but I loved the whole album.

There's a song on it called *Afraid.* It reminds me of the book *Found.* by T. Rigney. I wish I'd thought to bring that book because I feel like reading it now. It's brilliant.

Staying Up, by The Neighbourhood, is playing right now. This isn't a "park for a moment and write" song, so I've got to go, take advantage.

The point is… they're worth remembering. And I almost didn't get a chance to experience them. *Ever.* I feel grateful that they are two less in a billion good things I will not have had to miss out on.

In this situation, regret tries to take over one's thoughts. When someone feels they've lost control of their life, I think they fill their minds with looking backward... trying to fix what cannot be. Regret leaves people sitting dumbly on the side of a road, wishing they'd escaped with *just one* more person… and not feeling worthy of living because they didn't.

Some people need constant reassurance that their existence matters

12:44pm

I wish I knew how to siphon gas.

2:00pm

Ok. That sucked. In all ways.
I threw up—as if I can really afford to do that.

I pulled over to hit a small gas station/grocery.

I passed other stations that were bigger, links of big chains, but there were shitloads of vehicles at them and plenty of places for people to hide, but not me or anyone else approaching. Anyone hiding there they would have seen me coming from a quarter of a mile away, at least.

This place has woods nearby, which is not so cool, but it's virtually isolated. Probably a station that had been here for some time and made a large part of its business off of people who, just down the road, said, "Damn. We should have gassed up before we left town."

Another trick of the trade appeared to be from its overpriced groceries and souvenirs. The law of supply and demand says, when you're miles away from anywhere and you need TP or milk and eggs, you're going to pay for it like you *need* it.

The first thing that struck me when I entered the station was a peculiar, but not totally unfamiliar, smell of decay. It took a little while to locate the source. Then I found the tanks that were once full of living minnows and other bait.

It's actually a good thing for those tanks, because I wasn't having any luck finding something to work as a syphon. I figured the tubes that feed oxygen into the tanks would probably do the job.

I found a scissor and harvested the tubing sticking out of the rancid water. I don't know whether it was stupid or smart to have not taken chances with those other gas stations, but I had barely enough vapor in my tank to edge up next to the vehicle I was about to tap. I count myself fortunate that the car was old enough that I could just look and know how much was left in the tank. I'd gotten lucky.

After that foul sucking adventure was over, I ransacked the pre-sacked shop for something to clean my mouth—next time I know to stop before the gas reaches my mouth.

I found a partial roll of mints next to the register.

I swore all throughout the pilfered grocery, like I was christening it with profanity. There wasn't even anything for the dog.

I collected Minnesota, Illinois and Iowa road maps—along with my Wisconsin one, I think I'm set for a while. I sit for a while doodling. I remember the name of the state trooper. I wonder if he is alive.

I see no sign of busy bodies here, no dead bodies to speak of, besides the multitudes of animals, dead in the tanks. If it wouldn't be so stupid that I'd *deserve* to die, I'd like to sit out here and read a little while.

I need to get going again.

It's hard to travel, especially near the cities, where perpetual traffic jams block everything. There are wrecks to avoid and vehicles left in the middle of the road, undoubtedly because they ran out of gas and the driver wanted to gain every inch they could before running out of fumes. When they were forced to abandon that vehicle, who knows what was going on around them or what was coming for them.

I'm gonna figure out a system that works for getting around all the abandoned vehicles.
I *know*—no cities!

That's all I've got so far.

5:23pm

I pulled over because I had to pee. When I went around to the passenger side, Mr. Ages was wriggling like a puppy on espresso. I was apologizing for making him wait when he bolted out. I was left in his dust as he made after a raccoon.

"Are you fucking kidding me?" I groaned.

I went after him—I wanted to call him back, but I didn't dare yell. I heard him barking, but I couldn't see him.

Staring down the wooded acres, I hesitated. The barking seemed fainter. The next minute I'm slogging at full speed through cold, knee deep water, and up the other side of the ditch. My bladder jiggled heavily and painfully with every urgent step.

I chased for about a mile before he ran up from *behind* me with a look on his face like, "Where the hell have <u>you</u> been?"

I wanted to scream that he was bad. But instead I just walked past him, back toward the road.

Cheerfully, perhaps forcibly playful to make good for being a shithead, Mr. Ages danced beside me. My emotional mind saw the "Snoopy Dance" going on in my peripheral vision.

I remembered that the car was still running and, even as my lungs complained, I managed to work up to a jog.

By the time we got back and into the car, Mr. Ages probably felt like he was out of danger. He must have sensed I didn't have it in me to really punish him. Other times when he was bad he would slink like a lizard, tail waving or shaking more than wagging—everything about his face asserting how much he still loved me and if I loved him I wouldn't be mad. But instead he piled into his seat and stood facing me, looking pleased and stomping cheerfully, the bed of loose hairs he'd shed onto the upholstery.

Our eyes met. I was mad that he wasn't worried. I was furious at his wagging tail. And I was enraged at the joy in his eyes, the bow of his black lipped grin, the bounce in his hanging tongue, all equating the fact that he wasn't the least bit sorry.

"Don't ever leave me," was all I could choke out.

After a couple miles he got antsy and he kept walking in circles in the seat—his bum-hole pursing like kissy-lips.

"You are a <u>bad</u> dog!" I snapped.

I wanted to make him wait a while longer, but if he made a mess then I'd be punished by punishing him.

Then I remembered that *I* still had to piss.
Oh my God, I had to go!!

I braked hard and Mr. Ages poured into the floor space below the seat. I grabbed the accessible travel tissue pack and jumped out and "made due" behind the door, only after Mr. Ages shoved past me—nearly doing the splits as he went down hard on the gravel shoulder.

A little further off, back hunched up and tail pointing toward the sky he dropped a load. I didn't know dogs could get boners shitting. So fucking nasty!

We got back in the car.

I looked at the creature with whom I shared equal dependency. "You need to stay with me," I told him.

Oct 30 9:57am

Am at a state park.
I can't help thinking how close I am to where Marie lives.
Henry Ellis said: "All the art of living lies in a fine mingling of letting go and holding on."

There are some things I just can't let go of, not without knowing what happened.
There's something I can't know—not now.

I can't bear to.

Can I?

I struck out to search for my friends, or even my parents—who would I choose? How? Where would I begin? What were the chances that they'd still be at home, if they reached them at all?

Worst of all, how would I choose? The decision seems as important as picking one of them to survive. Why do I feel that way? Well, I know why... because they would be the one I knew was alive. ~~For everyone I love, all I have is hope, but there is a part of me that says that hope, in these circumstances, lives only in a fool.~~

My mind conjures enough horrible possibilities—realizing any of them really happened—no. I can't—I WON'T entertain the probability that—because I *don't* know. I can't know.

Why can't I be optimistic?

All these useless worries my heart or mind is holding onto…
they change nothing.

Mr. Ages killed a squirrel and a rabbit. He ate the squirrel. I
think the rabbit is for me???

I'm going to start a fire and hope we don't get any attention. It's
been quiet here, so far. I found some canned goods in the
campgrounds and Mr. Ages barked when there were busy
bodies—that high pitched bark/scream—as much an alarm as a
dinner bell…Ugh.

How miserable to be a dog - a good dog - and be afraid. It's
engrained in them to face the danger, the intruder, for us. They
aren't as selfish as people. Maybe they are, but they do what
we ask because they trust us so faithfully. If they think they are
loved, or respect their handler, do they really think that person
would put them in danger? Probably not…

Do we take advantage of their incredible loyalty? We ask them
to be our protectors and look after us… we expect them too,
even when they are of no size or skill to do it. We are
disappointed, irritated or amused when they bark at nothing,
because we have innate expectations of them.

I wonder what their expectations are of us.

What is a deal breaker for a dog? When do they lose faith in
us? Why did Mr. Ages approach me? Why has he stayed? Is it
just because I fed him, because I've had nothing for him in a
long time…

It's a really weird thing, trying to understand a dog, but it
doesn't feel impossible.

I'm going to boil some water because I don't have any. At least there were several cooking pots and stuff in camps. I'll boil it and fill my bottles when it cools.

Mr. Ages drank when we reached the creek—so I got my drinking water upstream. No offense Mr. Ages!

I'm taking the camping supplies I think I can use—most of it's pretty useful, actually. I got a Black Diamond LED headlamp. That could have been the only thing I found and I'd be delighted. *I* feel improved... not just my situation.

If or when someone reads this (if it's ever found) and things have improved, you might not know, understand or remember how much darker the world was when this was happening.

There are no far off glows of clustered buildings, streetlights, car lights, neon lights. There are no random lights on in the middle of the night where you wonder who is up and why would they be, at this hour. There's nothing in the night, but stars and moonlight.

The air is like ink and the animals in it are excited by the news that they own the world again.

Amongst the sounds, it's easy to lose track of what's moving where.

Depth perception? Forget it.
Not in this "new night"...
Last night I pounced on the dark with my flashlight blazing because I heard "something."

Where the beam pooled, I found a gnarled tree… it was just a tree… until I turned my attention elsewhere. I reeled back, turning hard on my heel, finally processing what comprised the tree's skin. I'd seen the skeletally thin busy body, but it hadn't registered—flattened against, clutching, the gray and ragged as bark. Only then it was slinking toward me.

11:20am

Had salt and pepper from a camp—the rabbit was pretty good. Considering the things I've seen, I'm proud of myself for being able to stomach cleaning it, much less eating it. I'm proud of myself for not thinking about the feel of my teeth against its bones. Or the texture of the sinewy muscle as my incisors cut it or my canines tear it. Getting beyond the way, when it was on the spit and cooking, that it looked like a little human body.

I don't really know how.

I think I blocked out everything until my hunger was sated, because I'm feeling a little sick now.

Mr. Ages got the guts. He'd probably eat the fur too—he was definitely interested, but I put it in someone's suitcase so he couldn't get at it. I don't know that it would hurt him – there is probably a lot of nutrition in the skin… it's the aftermath of all that fur I want to spare him of. His droppings would look like owl pellets… I can't imagine it would feel that great coming out either.

I watch him cleaning himself after his meal, generously addressing his paws. His ears swiveling, always on duty. I pity him. I cannot explain any of this to him. Does he pity me? He cannot explain it to me either.

I'm not alone in this. He is every bit like me, in this terrible way.

I wonder what his life was like.
What was his name?
Was he bought, born, or adopted into his family?
Who was/were his master(s)? . . . Does he think about them?

It's not as obvious anymore, having been together this long, but it *was* obvious he missed something. I could see it in his eyes, in his body language, when there was still hope… when he was looking for something. Or waiting for someone… When I put my hand on him and he crushes his head or shoulder into my palm, I know, he remembered being pet that way. He was getting a little more out of it than just my affection. I felt like he was trying to reclaim something, someone.

Separation from me is hard on him.

He was so frantic when I came back with the car.

I look down at him. I watch him. I pay attention to the way he responds to every night sound, every day sound. I pay attention to how he pays attention to me. How, when we walk together, he swings his head up to look at me, to watch me. He watches everything I do. He pays attention to how I respond to every night sound, every day sound.

I'm afraid to love him. He's not afraid of anything, especially not that. He loves without consideration of self or even reciprocation of love. Animals are like that.

He needs me.

I have never been anyone's "world entire"…until now.

1:29pm

I wish I'd done at <u>my</u> house what I did at the second place I stayed—the place I just abandoned. There, I left the key in the door, in case someone else came by.
But when I left my home I hadn't intended on never returning.

How many people is that true for?

Oct 31 8:41am - HAPPY HALLOWEEN!

I got a treat—only one pack of graham crackers was missing from the box. It wasn't even open!

Something got into the marshmallows that had been in there— maybe even Mr. Ages.

I heard him grunt with effort when he was trying to poop this morning. Ha Ha!
As for me—knock on wood.
No tricks yet.

This place is a treasure trove. I'll never be able to check everything. I would, if I could stay. It would take a long time to get through everything—this is paradise for the living.

Everything here was meant for living away from home. I have no idea what that may all entail, but what I'm finding so far is going to make life a lot easier for me.

I'd love an RV—there are a couple nice looking ones here—with gas!

Three problems:

*There might not be keys
*Maneuvering them between vehicles—driving them at all!
*The MPG

Don't even have to think about the other problems after the first.

Am going to do one more sweep for supplies and move out. I have acquired a nice mess kit, canteen, a variety of matches and lighters, a few small bricks (the size of candy bars) which are supposed to help ignite campfires and charcoal. Canned goods, a nice tong, a little flour and spices, among a few other odds and ends.

So far Halloween has been a lot more treats than tricks.

P.S. So far nothing *weird*—or do I have to wait until evening? Are you superstitious? Most the time I'm not. I used to only entertain the idea of ghosts and crap when it was fun.
Is it stupid? I'm actually pretty nervous.
Some people, as you probably know, believe that today, like Dia de los Muertos, the dead are free to roam the earth.

They're pretty damn liberated already, if you ask me... so...
What the fuck are they going to do today??

11:50am

I couldn't leave it alone.

I came across a familiar road. The green street sign and white letters cried for my attention, like a desperate hitchhiker. I didn't slow down at first… at first I only wondered if it could, somehow, be the same road… how many roads are there with this name? Could it be the same road… that which would, eventually, lead any traveler within a mile and a half of the little dirt, country road to Marie's home?

My foot had come off the gas, and hovered over the accelerator. Slowly it reached for the brake, but the car was barely crawling. I put the car in park, relocked the doors, and with trembling hands, unfolded the Iowa road map. I followed the highway to that county road and followed its path west. The paper felt rough under my finger. It hissed against the map as it glided along the black line.

Somewhere down that strange road it would merge with the portion of it I'd driven dozens of times in the past. It'd reach the houses I coveted. Towns I thought were lovely. Businesses I recognized. Places destined to strike me as both horrible and wonderful for the same reason, because they were familiar.

At the end of those conversant miles would be a house… even more familiar.

Hunched over the map, when I looked up, my gaze barely cleared the dashboard. All I saw were the top halves of trees. I sat up straight and looked at the unremarkable countryside— absent for the first time, in probably a century or more, was the odor of pig farms and turned soil. It was a place in transition. Deceptively still, considering how quickly it was going feral.

I felt something out there calling to me. Almost, I think, I heard my name. It was telling me this was the last chance I'd ever have... that I would never come this way again.

-

It was eerie pulling into that driveway.
I didn't want to look at it, lest I should *see*: vandalism, blood, bodies or zombies. Just seeing a yard that was always cared for being neglected was an unignorable headline that everything had changed.

I got out, leaving the door barely ajar. My eyes fixed on the dirt. I expected the screen door to slam and Marie's loud voice greeting me with affectionate profanity and soft, warm arms around me. While the vision was so clear, I could almost smell her hair, when we hugged—an ugly thing overcame the memory of how it always was before... In it, the screen door banged. Marie burst out on the front steps, arms hanging low and limply at her sides, being led by her mouth, which was torn to one ear... and that loose skin pulled back like it was being drawn into a ponytail. Her shoulder meat was eaten down to the bone. And in that vision I notice that all the bites on her are small. Just as I wonder where the kids are, from under the car something grabs my foot.

I recoil from the car and from the vision. I feel where my foot had been grabbed before and grind at the sensation with my other foot, like I was putting out a cigarette.

I wait a moment longer, but only silence greets me.

I turned my back on the house to use the hood of my car to write a note to this friend I'd known for decades.

I don't know if she was there. I don't want to know—unless I could know they were okay. If she is not, I don't know that I could do what I should… for my own safety or her own good.

My sight is blurring and the writing is dancing like water. I blink away the tears to clear them. They leave three gray suns on the paper. The eraser is black and hard. It would do more harm than good. I am careful to say all I need to.

If she's wondering, then she'll at least know I *am*.

As I wrote, I was *sure* I heard a voice beckon me to turn around. The hair stood up on the back of my neck. The call was strong enough, the voice so real, that I involuntarily turned my head a little—despite that I readily resisted it.
I used a couple bandages to hang the note on the mailbox and edged toward the car, with my back to the house.

The Something called to me more urgently.

It said, in a voice I *really* heard, "You'll never know, unless you know."

I closed the car door and locked it. Only then did I allow myself to look for the source. Eight black eyes of the double garage door stared at me. Terrified me.

I lost a little time then—the next thing I remember I was turning off the dirt road and heading back to the last point of my intended path.

I would never go anywhere near there again.

"I can't!" I cried out to no one and everything.
Mr. Ages stared at me.

My hands shook uncontrollably on the wheel. The trembling worked up my arms. Something moved in my gut, bouncing and pawing, pittering and pattering—like I'd swallowed something alive. It began climbing my throat.

My friends.

My friends.

　　My friends.

I couldn't hold my head steady.

My vision blurred, but it was okay. I was going back the way I came—I felt confident in remembering what was on the road and of being alone in it—and, at that time, being alone in the whole world.

I couldn't listen to the voice.
I wailed, driving the air out of my lungs until they were raw.
My fists shook the wheel.
Don't even know how I was driving.
I could never do what it wanted.
I wouldn't look.
I *couldn't* look.

What if her car wasn't in the garage?

9:26pm

I missed the state line via little back roads. I *think*.
I don't know where I am. Car said I was heading south.
I stopped to let out Mr. Ages—

—someone shot at me.

I didn't know what to do.

Yell?

Say, "Hey, I'm alive—don't shoot!"

If you've seen the same movies I have you'd just haul ass, like I did.

If they are bad—I hope I'm not going toward them.

If they are good... I dunno.

If they are somewhere in between—which is really most likely...

Okay, but the asshole *shot* at me.

How many zombies travel with dogs???

Nov 1 4:04pm

I sped away from there.

The ring of metal deflecting off the asphalt beside me still resonates in my mind. ka-PING! That and, "What the fuck?!?"

I'm needing gas again, but decide to lay low and think before I do anything hasty—like continuing to run away when the shooter might not give a damn who I was or where I went. If they were on foot, they'd be hard pressed to come after me. I could be racing past important things... I just need to think.

Unfortunately I'm not thinking of anything worthwhile.

Want to know how my cognitive ability is being used? Strictly for distraction. Refusing to be here and now. Myself and I are playing my favorite survivor game...

Okay—in *Dawn of the Dead*, after the douche, prick, coward Stephen is dead *and if* Roger hadn't been bit, I could ride this out with them. I think they're the best group I can think of from a post-apocalyptic movie. I guess there are a couple others I wouldn't mind. The good guys in *The Stand* would be the best *community* to be with.

There's usually someone in a group that ruins it for me. I couldn't just enter the group and beat their ass because I *know* what kind of person they really are. Then I would have to explain my psychic abilities. hahaha

Do you ever ask yourself "if" questions?

I often I ask myself those kind of questions to occupy my mind. That particular "if" is one of my favorites because I always forget people or groups that I like. For instance, I just remembered another group of apocalypse survivors, though, to be honest I'd probably take my chances of alienating myself from the rest of the group by killing a couple of them.

I say that like I think it would be easy to kill someone.

With some people… I think, yes—if there were no consequences—in a freaking heartbeat. I can say that, but would I really? I don't know. "I hate" that—and "I wish they were dead"—and "I could just kill" so-and-so—come out of our mouths and go into our heads so easily. It's no wonder then that the collapse of society should lead to a derailment of morality.

Is it possible to think about society, about right and wrong, good and bad, regret and consequences without thinking of *him*?

Not yet.

If his uncle were standing in front of me—I would shoot him. No. I would drive my hammer into his skull and tie him up while he was unconscious. When he came to, starting with his toes, I'd start smashing my way up his body.

Would I really?

Honestly...?   I think so.

So...

If I get tired of that "if" scenario, I also entertain myself with:

"If I could eat anything right now, what would it be?"

- or -

-"If there was a theme song for the end of the world, what would it be?"

I think *In Avernus*, by Nothingface. I get it in my head all the time. Not incidentally either, I think it's environmental... I bet you'd have trouble beating it. Sometimes it feels like torture. Sometimes like comfort.

- If I found the perfect place to make a go of it, in this situation, what would it have to have?

Water. A sound shelter. A long growing season. A fireplace or a generator. Bookshelves...

- If I could choose one occupation or skill what would be the most useful in this situation, what would it be?

Never been able to decide.

-If I was stuck in a zombie apocalypse with one person living or dead, who would it be. OR - would I rather it was this person or that person?

And you can do *that* two ways—to switch it up. I sometimes choose between two people I'd hate to be stuck with or two people that I think it might be okay—most the time I choose fictional people—

- or -

I can change how many people are involved. Or have groups like: Would I rather be in a zombie apocalypse if I HAD to— with the *Golden Girls* or the *Designing Women*?

I'm sure you got it before the example.

There are worse things I could think about.
Worse things I could do with my time.

I read whenever I can.
The Road is dog-eared on pages where there's a thought or phrase with new meaning or importance. It's dog-eared at moments I can't help but return to, for whatever reason.

I never treated books like that before, or rather I haven't since junior high when I supplemented my dystopian reading with a growing curiosity for romance novels, dog-earing the "good parts". My copy of *The Road* is starting to looks as much a survivor as myself.

I draw sometimes, but I didn't think to bring a sketch pad.

Most days I take out my photos and spend some time on the importance of remembering.

Nov 3 1:49am

I parked by a couple of broke down/abandoned vehicles. My car's almost out of gas. Making sounds like "Gug" "Gug" "Gug" and the fuel light's been on for a while. I didn't want to wander around in the dark. Have had the nagging feeling that I am not alone.

Will take care of it in the morning.

I wish I knew where I'm going to end up so I knew to head there.

Lewis Carroll wrote:

"If you don't know where you are going, any road will get you there."

I guess that's okay, as long as it's southbound.

To be honest, I said, "Fuck it" to the quest for gas earlier today, when I went for the handle of the nearest vehicle and my fingers pressed into the soft, bulbous abdomen of an orb spider. It's the size of a robin egg—pale and striped. I took a twig and tried to flick it out without popping it. I ended up impaling it.

Jee-sus!

I still feel fucking crawly when I think of its goddamn legs moving.

Nov 5 9:53pm

While the sun was setting I still couldn't see anything on the hillside, even though it was jet black against the hot yellow light.

When twilight cast that reality blurring, bluish gray half-night over the everlasting unfamiliar, I wasn't sure what I was seeing.

But when night fell, I was certain. Below the faintest whisper of smoke was a distant campfire. A fire, so small and far away it twinkled like a star.

How I wonder what you are...

Nov 6 4:26am

I found a busy body in a hatchback about 15 minutes ago. My flashlight caught the movement before I heard it thumping around inside. Mr. Ages' bark sounded like bad brakes, getting louder and fast as we approached. I wished he wouldn't... night had long since fallen and my ears were playing tricks on me. Under the sound of his barking, one would not even have to sneak to get close to us. If the spotlight from the flashlight were not directly on them, the darkness was a veil of invisibility... would the dog be too distracted to notice?

I was already cold, but a different kind of chill entered me One that no amount of clothes, shelter, or heat could chase out...

The busy body was pacing like a tiger in a cage.

I didn't want to think about it then, but I guess I am willing to write it now—based on the items I could see through the glass, sleeping bag and pack, flashlight, hiking stick, and a baseball bat—I think he was just like me.

I never want to be like that.

There was a roll of duct tape amongst the visible possessions. Some of the sheets he'd taped up on the windows were still hanging in the front, where his corpse, apparently, never wandered.

I saw a bite in the meat of his lower arm. There might have been claw marks on his arm. He was half-dressed. I couldn't see any other bites. All the other wounds were just from his flesh rotting.

It was not so easy to imagine the man as he was when he was living, but probably only a week ago, or so, he was. And, if I had to guess, I'd say he narrowly escaped a great many more bites—suffering the only one that mattered as a dead thing clawed at his arm to grasp it.

I slowly started away, looking back at him through quite a few of the first steps.

He didn't stop moving. He crawled faster.

Somehow his dead eyes never left me, even as his routine forced him to turn his back on me. His head wrapped around until it rest his chin on his back…

I must have been seeing things.

Nov 7 8:20pm

Another early morning. Yuck.

I was too nervous to stay asleep.

I watched the sun set from an overpass. Witnessed the three dimensional world transform into silhouette. All too soon, with impossible speed, the night engulfed the day in perfect, tar thick darkness.

It was at this point when I saw the UFO.

Its silvery pot pie shaped mass floated toward me over the trees, making sounds a child would make for a ghost, only higher. Its movements were as realistic as fake boobs.

…

…

…in other words—nothing happened today worth writing.

Nov 8 4:51pm

I caught myself feeling good today. Sincerely. Absolutely. Amazingly good…

We were just walking. And that's *exactly* what it felt like we were doing. Just taking a walk... I had the feeling that, at any driveway, I should sense we were home and go there. The sour stink of death was conspicuously absent. So were the wrecks and litter.

I realized I was singing to myself. *Crossroads,* by Matisyahu, like the acoustic version. Ahh, I love it! I wasn't thinking about how loud I was. I was lost in Oz and Dorothy's dismal gray somewhere was nowhere. Somehow—I found perfect harmony with the world—as is.

His work can make a person feel that way.

Anyway, it was…….uplifting.

How can I describe how amazing it felt to feel, if only for a moment, that everything was normal?

Good God.

I took so much for granted.

Nov 14 9:34pm

Moonlight struck every hump of the rolling and rising country road before me. Only for that moonlight did I see the thriving nightmare pour over the greatest of the hills.

A slow moving wave ate up the blacktop, still shiny from an earlier rain shower. I imagined it like a tsunami—a wall of death that was definitely moving faster than it looked.

I shrugged on the strap of my bag and held it on my shoulder with the hand that, unconsciously, took up the hammer.

Mr. Ages anxiously looked up at me. I pet him.

I felt the handle of the screwdriver tap my wrist when my hand settled at my side. What I'd have given that it was the handle of a gun instead...

Rising from the bottom of the hill nearest to me, came something like a man whose entire flesh was the off color of a bad bruise. More than blood, a pus-like fluid quivered like cold fat on the mouth of every wound. Flies lit on the horde so densely that I could see them in the dark. I heard them where I couldn't see them.

Half a dozen more were coming over the next hill.

They were coming out of the woods.

A head, neck, shoulder, and arm were all that was left of a woman coming up along the ditch. Her organs and entrails made crude tentacles behind her, like some kind of sea witch. Another, maybe it was a man before, was only a creature of protruding and splintered bones and shredded flesh now.

None terrified me as much as this closest rotting thing.

I felt like I was facing down the Horseman of Pestilence. The sensation of falling filled my head. I tried to stop myself, but I was still standing. Color drained out of everything before my eyes.

I almost fainted. That scared me so bad—I became alert like God had slapped me.

Maybe He did.

There was no way to win.

Shit.

This one—this horrible One.

Something told me I couldn't—maybe nothing—could stop him.

I wound my arm and hand into Mr. Ages' leash so he'd have to break it off before I'd lose him. I didn't say anything to comfort or control him. I was afraid they were already too aware of me.

That one… I *know* saw me. The damn thing looked right in my eyes.

Can the dead see?

I led Mr. Ages off the road and started running. No doubt, dragging the dog sometimes.

The tall wet grass quickly soaked me. It was cold. I was shaking, but it had nothing to do with that. To my left, I heard them crunching through the woods. I heard the disgusting sounds they make.

I smelled them everywhere.

Mr. Ages started making high pitched yips. Without thinking, scared shitless, I snapped at him to shut up—and not quietly.

My shoulder bounced off something soft. It made a guttural sound.
I heard hooved things running.

A flourish of beating wings exploded through the air around me when I charged through a cluster of scratchy bushes.

I thought I felt something grab my sleeve—tug at my pack—

It was so fucking dark!

The woods were dangerous—easy to get lost—easy to get hurt.

I felt like I ran forever.

I was being slapped and scratched, hopefully not by them. I feared holes, old wells, dried creek beds, stray lines of barbed wire from old property lines…

The forest puked me out in a field.

I saw a farm. Beyond it lay another road that I wouldn't know about until the morning. There were several buildings on the property. We ran to what was probably the original farmhouse, an abandoned building that sat amongst a heap of junk.

I broke out a small window to get in. I hoisted Mr. Ages through it. Nothing but pigeons and spiders had been anywhere near this place in years.

There was a small loft with a ladder. I drug the poor yipping mutt up there and brought the ladder up behind us. I took the leash's end and wrapped it around his mug. Then crushed him with my body to keep him still.

It might not have been the first undead to reach the farm, but I saw when the first busy body, I knew of, found the window. I saw its silhouette block out the moonlight. It stuck its head through and stuffed its head, on what looked like a too-long neck, through the space.

We lay in the thick smell of mildew and listened to the dead passing us by. The one at the window didn't move. It just made an "Awwwwww" sound all night long, on what could have been one breath—if they breathed. *All* night long...
I "killed" it this morning.

When finally we went out, all that was left of the herd was a somewhat trampled field and their stench.

I hadn't remembered crossing any remnants of a fence and yet there it was. I hadn't remembered being hurt, and yet my being was riddled with raised and bloody hashtags brought by angry branches and, maybe, boards. The stink of mold and dust lay on us, but did not register until the morning breeze ran over us. Where to go next, was the all-important question. After excluding the possibility of returning to the road on the other side of the woods, there was only that which lay on the other side of the field. So that is what we struck out for.

In my ears, there was only the sound of the uncut straw sweeping across my legs, until a line of geese came calling loudly overhead. I raised my eyes to see them and something else caught my attention.

On the fringe of the woods opposite us, beyond another small field, there was a zombie. Even from this distance and without my contacts in or glasses on, I knew which one it was.

He that did not stumble or stagger, despite being ravaged by decomposition. He whose eyes were full of cunning, instead of the strange emptiness that likens itself only to the famished. He went out before the horde of them like their leader. He was different.

He was *wrong*…

I hate to even write about it.
Like bringing him up will conjure him.
It makes me sick to even thinking about him out *there*. Like a huge spider in your house that you've tried to kill, but it manages to drag itself into a vent or something and you don't know if it's hurt enough that it won't come back. Wondering where it is and what it's doing and when or if you'll see it again.

Never would be too soon.

Nov 28 7:09am

It's been hard to find a good place to sit and write. I'd run into some bad weather—as if I just turned down the wrong road. ☺

Freezing rain put about 1/4 an inch of crystal clear Unmanageable on everything.

Okay, I had to look back; I forgot what I'd last wrote you. Wrote me?

So you should already know, or guessed, my car wouldn't start—even when I got it some gas. After I'd got past the spider incident... Of course, I can't hotwire cars. So that's why we've, obviously, been walking since then.

It hasn't been great, because of the barking, but at least he doesn't do it if they aren't close to us—like outside of 500 feet. I wish I had better shoes.

Well—there are a lot of things that I'd have if I could.

Right now my heart's with a baked potato with real butter and a sprinkle of pepper, a rare steak smothered in mushrooms, caramelized onions, and a bowl of vanilla ice-cream with pineapples on top and on the side. And a beer... a Bud Light, so chilled it has frost on it.

And, for some reason, my heart's longing for *him*.

-

In some ways travelling on foot is great, but I yearn to go faster. I feel like I'm late to be somewhere or maybe I feel urgent to get somewhere and claim it for myself.

I've decided, if I can make it halfway south, I will have the best chance to make a go of it. I need to avoid "real" winters.

I realized I might stand a good chance of being able to squirrel away some seeds, if I can find them. I expect there to be plenty in stores, since all this started around the beginning of June.

Maybe it didn't for other people.

Who knows what other people were told was happening.
I guess the real question is when it became real for each of us.

As I write this, I'm sitting at someone's kitchen table.
I did some significant damage breaking in—I can't stay long.

I needed to rest and a chance to sort out my thoughts.
I talk to myself and Mr. Ages too much—so much that I worry.
I don't know much about psychology, but I find myself
muttering about what I'm doing. I don't have any reason to talk.

When I *don't* talk, I'm stuck in here where all this writing comes from.

Sometimes I shiver like I'm cold—and I'm not.
Blood sugar?
Are my nerves giving out? My sanity?

Am I lucid enough to know if something's wrong?

Can you worry so much about going crazy that you do?

Am I a boiler that needs to vent and won't?
What do I vent?
How?

Sometimes I feel like I'm going to break down. I'll think I'm fine—I'm not thinking about anything at all—then, suddenly, I can barely walk. Then I can't breathe and I'm somewhere between sobbing and puking.

Other times, I feel like all I want to do is stand still and scream as loud as I can for as long as I can… and do that over and over and over again.

Sometimes I lose time. I lose miles. My mind leaves me on auto pilot.

Every time I regain control, Mr. Ages is standing there, pressed against me. Worrying –I don't *imagine* that he worries.

And he gets sad.

He gets sleepy.
He can be playful—sometimes he's so nuts it's like a caffeine crab has clamped on his ass.
He's feeling this, just like me.

He's lost just as much as us—everything he knew. And, like me, he probably doesn't know what happened to whoever he loved. Or, maybe worse than that, he knows exactly what happened to them…

On the bright side—we're now living it up.
Do you know how long Slim Fast stays fresh?
A long time. And it doesn't need refrigeration.
I don't know a lot about nutrition, but there are tons of vitamins and crap in these. I'm sure all stuff I could use.
There are four cases in the pantry and two bottles in the fridge: 34 bottles = 34 meals.

I also got a bunch of vitamins and I'm boiling water on the barbeque out front to make noodles. Macaroni and cheese, if the powder packet is still good—I'm gonna eat it no matter, but I *thought* I checked it.

I have three more boxes of that and some oatmeal.

The couple that lived here must have planned to wait it out. They had it barricaded pretty well. There are public notice fliers for going to the nearest "Relief Station" on the corkboard by the phone, but I can't imagine that they'd leave this for something unknown.

I wonder what happened to them.

Janice and Mickey Wright.

They have a lot of pictures on their walls.

They are probably in their 50's. They look like nice people.

Stuffing my face with their food—I can't help but like them.

No pictures of children, but a lot of cats. I haven't seen any, but Mr. Ages will eat well on their food.

I can't stay because of what I did to the door. I'd have to seal it off to keep it closed and I have no idea how to do that. That's no good.

After the noodles are done I'll do the best I can, basically a half-assed job making it secure so I don't have to worry about anything coming in while I'm eating.

I need to find a way to move all this stuff. The burden of water is load enough. I don't want to leave any of this. There'll be hell to pay first.

I take a deck of cards.

I was hoping for a rifle.

I can hear Mr. Ages crunching on dry cat food while I'm writing at the kitchen table in this cute little one bedroom house.

If the windows weren't boarded over—neatly, I think I should point out—this would have a very "normal" feel to it.

When the water boils I'm going to have a cup of instant coffee with sugar—I hate dried creamer.
I already went through the caffeine withdrawal—I don't know if I really need to get into that again, but I'm going to.
I'm very willfully falling off the wagon.

Earlier, while waiting for things to cook, I'd been sitting at the table, nibbling on some Extreme Cheddar snack crackers—of which age seems to not matter. I caught a glimpse of myself in the tall glass panes of a hutch. My hands were near my mouth. My eyes looked particularly dark and large, hovering over my fingertips. I thought again how much we are kindred to rats... but it gave me no pleasure to think it. I am doing well for the moment. It makes me sad to think how much better that might be than many others are. I will not find any home stocked by an apocalypse preparedness zealot or decked out fallout shelter... This is Lady Luck on her back, legs spread and giving everything she's got... anything more is a pipedream.

Tonight, I hope everyone's doing this well.

Nov 29 6:46am

Mankind can do just about anything. We could adapt if God flooded the world again. We could adapt to anything that 150 years ago would have devastated mankind.
Is this the length God had to go to?

Or is this a way to start over, for us, as a species—I am content to think that.
Maybe then I wouldn't have any reason to worry about the people I love.

Maybe this is Armageddon.
Maybe all the pieces of shit are dead and dragged down to Hell because there's nothing to debate. The Purge…

So maybe all the really good people have gone ahead because God *knew* they were good, without a doubt.
Maybe, with everyone that's left, there is some doubt about where we belong and we're being tested to see how we really rate.

I accept the challenge. I need something to work toward.

-

Though there are things I've told myself I *had* to do that I'm not happy about. Things that, never in my life, did I think I would do…

I don't want to live this and then go to Hell too.

Do you believe in a higher power?
Do you believe in God?
I do.
With how fucked up things are, I wouldn't take any chances.
And what's the harm?
False hope? Is there such a thing?
I wonder how many people of faith or otherwise are having doubts they never had before.

I find myself thinking about God more than I have in years.

I used to pray when luck was walking a razor's edge and I hoped He'd tip things in my favor—or at least without being cut too bad.

I'd pray when I thought it'd maybe been too long since I had.

I haven't been to church since 5th grade.
I don't feel I <u>need</u> to attend to be as good as anyone that does. To me, the core of what most religions want is merely for us to not be pieces of shit. Call it playing it safe—or call it commonsense theology—or how about a little common decency.

I think gods were conjured from suffering—when people needed something for hope—which is what keeps us going, isn't it? Gods also give us something to blame …

Because sometimes it's really hard to be human.

It's no wonder then, why I've thought so much about these things.

If God *is* undecided about everyone that's still alive—I've sometimes wondered if Mr. Ages is some kind of emissary or supervisor. Maybe there's a grosbeak that's following the person that shot at me and is reporting back what a son-of-a-bitch they are.

If that's what's going on, then God's "soul inspector" just rolled over to clean himself.

I doubt this is the first time I've seen him from this angle, but it's clear that he's been neutered. My gut tells me he was cared for.

In a second here, I'm going to get up to boil some more water—I'm thinking oatmeal.
There are supplies here—more than I can take. But I can't stay.

The rest? It'll be here for the next person.

Found a large rolling suitcase for my food supply—will significantly lighten my pack—all but a soda bottle's worth of water that I'm going to keep on me.

9:37 am

I slept too hard—I'm sure Mr. Ages must have barked. I can't believe he would not have noticed…

We had about an inch of snow and hoarfrost this morning. There, unmistakably—evidence someone had come by this morning, before I woke at 5-ish. 5:11—Not only passed by, but worse…

Out on the road, I stood staring in disbelief at where the snow and ice melted back in a plate sized circle and left the snow around it dirty—gray and brown.
A vehicle had idled there.

Suddenly I heard an engine turn over somewhere behind a neighbor's house, where someone could easily watch us.

My heart filled my throat, I choked. Mr. Ages growled deeply. *Oh my God*, I thought:

They're coming.

Dec 15 2:44pm

I locked Mr. Ages in the bathroom and used my claw hammer
to take the boards off the bathroom window, which I found
shattered, once I broke through.
A hidden part of me was taking over… autopilot…the refusal,
not of dying, but of dying badly. Of being a prisoner and
whatever lot is drawn along with that… I surprise myself with
strength, speed and deliberate action—an undisclosed plan.

Mr. Ages was instantly upset—I was going out that window
and he knew it.

Don't leave me! Don't leave me! Don't leave me! I heard—not
barking.

I couldn't see him from the ground—where I landed hard—but
I know what a dog looks like who wants out or wants
something more than life itself. He was hysterical—barking
and yipping, howling madly.
Screaming.

I picked myself up.
I heard a car door close.
Then I heard a second.

I was going deaf again—both loud and silent humming in my
head—maybe buzzing—something felt not heard. But I could
feel my pulse in every fiber of muscle, in every nerve. My flesh
got cold, not just because it was cold—I didn't have my coat.

All my things, but my tools, were in the bathtub.

A one-armed woman, undead, was in the backyard—she was moving too slowly to worry about, right then—but I didn't dare forget about her or turn my back on her too long.

Sometimes they move faster than you think they can.

I peeked around the corner and then slid into the path my eyes had just scanned with satisfaction. No one was there.

Behind me, I saw movement out of the corner of my eye—a man came into the backyard. If there were two people, I was <u>fucked</u>. They would be able to see, in the snow, that someone had escaped from the window. If they wanted to find me, they would only have to move in opposite directions.

Mr. Ages noticed the man too. I never heard him bark like that.

Standing close to the siding, the vinyl panels cold against the nape of my neck, the back of my hands, I thought about a game I played when I was kid—Ten Steps Around the House.

All ye, All ye outs in free!

"Hey bitch!" I heard him say to the busy body. I heard him hock a loogie. He must have been sick, still struggling to clear his throat when he added, "Aww baby, let's get a look at you, baby."

I heard him let out a startled, "Whoa!" Must have been too close…or she was quicker than he expected.

And I guess, when I wondered how I would know if someone was good or bad I didn't expect it to be that easy. I was only half grateful, because there was no way around dealing with it.

Dealing with someone…

A weak chest-burster hammered against my ribs. My head buzzed like it was full of wasps. I heard him holler to someone else—"Did you get her yet? Wait 'til you see what I found back here!"

"You're fresh enough for me," he said to the dead woman.

"And you're dead motherfucker," I promised, no louder than a breath.

I heard someone at the front door, but only my soul took the time to feel relief. If they were trying to break in they wouldn't have to try hard. They were not knocking, not calling ahead, not afraid at all…

They were in by the time I reached the front door.

I didn't think too much about the rest. I couldn't.

I rushed in behind him. He would expect the other guy—since they both expected me to still be inside—me, with the dog barking, behind a locked door, trapped like rats.

I stuck the screwdriver into his throat with my right hand and let go. I knew he'd turn on me, no matter how surprised he was or how bad it hurt. Adrenaline considered, I wonder if it hurt at all.

It wouldn't have a chance to.

He had a handgun. I grabbed that wrist—my hammer finished him.

I retrieved my screwdriver and blood shot out across the floor at my feet. Then I noticed blood on my hands. I was hurt from crawling through the broken window. My arms were shredded. Adrenaline considered; I didn't feel much at all.

"Hey, I think there's a Stinker in here!" the other man hollered. He was walking around the side of the house—following my blood.

I panicked, driving the screwdriver into the dead man's ear before he "came back". I had only a breath or two before the second man reached me.

The tip of a rifle moved through the broken front door. I turned the hammer's claw into the mid-forearm of its bearer and plunged the screwdriver deep into the man's eye.

When he dropped, I kept my hold on the screwdriver and he slipped off it and down the four steps outside. I went down with him because the claw of the hammer was stuck in his arm.

I heard running on the frost and snow—there was a shrill cry— a woman flung herself on me.
She was skinny and seemed impossibly light, even so, the fight was pretty matched until she bit me—*I* screamed.
I went berserk.

The next thing I knew I was out in the backyard. I was stepping over the one-armed busy body. I knew I'd killed it because I could smell the odor of death on the tools I carried. I was disoriented. Didn't know where I was going… I turned around and went clumsily back to the front yard, using the house to keep me standing. In the back of my mind, the sound of the screwdriver dragging across the wall.

I went to their car and through their things. They didn't have much ammo, but it was better than nothing.

I took the rifle and handgun and checked their bodies for anything useful—I took the car keys.
I broke out the house's back door.
I got my things.
I got my dog.

Mr. Ages didn't settle down for hours. Panting, yipping, jumping against the dash. Restlessly turning circles in the seat and on the floor. Jumping up. Jumping down. Stumbling into the back seat, looking out windows. Pacing behind me. Scrambling to the front seat. Checking me. That I'm still here. I'm *still* here. Yes, still here…

It took hours for me to feel like we were "far enough away". Then I needed to stop and digest what just happened to us.

That was when I noticed the knife in my shoulder. I yanked it out, chucked it out, put the car in park and lifted my leaden foot off the brake.

I don't know how to describe the sound that came out of my throat. My hands flew to my face. I threw my head back and let it out. When it was done, my throat was hoarse. Even my breath was raspy.

I turned to Mr. Ages. I looked expectant. He wagged his tail. Then my arms were full of him.
I hugged him hard.

I wish he could have understood why I'd left him, how sorry I was that it scared him.

I don't know how long I held him—just until I noticed how much blood I was getting on him and how dizzy I felt.
I barely managed to cover the wounds before I passed out.
When I woke up, the car was out of gas.

I don't know how much blood I lost.
I am sick. And terrified—having had one too many hours to contemplate if I'd be a busy body soon. The fever didn't help— my reasoning or my fear.

I ditched the car after I came around. We managed to keep all our supplies.

We found ourselves on a stretch of four-lane littered with vehicles heading north.. a few, broke down, on the south facing lanes… no houses, or even buildings, as far as I could see.

Cars get picked over probably more than homes or stores— because there's more of them and it's safer. So I don't like to sleep in them. I feel justified in my concern that someone may try to get in it. I'd be a sitting duck… Blood loss and a fever didn't give me much choice.

I found shelter by colliding into it.

I had no other sense it existed.

I slid along the side of the minivan until I found a door handle. It felt like five hundred pounds as I pulled it back on its track. My shoulder screamed. I operated on tunnel vision and what world I was aware of was colorless. Unconsciousness overtook me like a brigand. With little time to spare, I put down the backseats, locked up and lay down in the bed I made.

I lost a lot of days.

I'm glad my watch keeps track of dates or else how would I know how many? What does that help me? I can't do anything about it. In fact, it made me more worried than if I'd awakened after those days and thought I'd just lost hours.

I feel really pathetic when I think about how my watch's battery dying will upset me as bad as I'm afraid it will.

Mr. Ages messed himself in the van multiple times, but I wasn't always clear enough to let him out. When I was conscious, he needed water and food—so did I.

She had a knife when she jumped on me. I never saw it. I didn't feel when it was buried in me…

I killed three people—easily.

I was scared out of my mind, but I think it should have been harder.

The busy body in the backyard had been dressed when I first saw her, hadn't she? I think it was a tawny plaid shirt… When I stepped over her she wasn't. I heard what he said. I've seen enough apocalypse movies to know...
I'll never be sorry about killing him.

I know now what would happen if I came across other survivors.

I don't know what to feel about it.

Dec 16 7:16am

When I was fourteen I found a dead person.

It was spring thaw and the snow receded enough that the shape of the exposed ground around him looked like a gingerbread man.
I knew who he was.

I'd never met him. I couldn't and can't even remember his name, but I remember all the articles and the news about the missing hunter.

The blaze orange jacket was in ribbons. He'd been eaten on—a lot. The claw marks were clear. Bites that weren't successful enough to tear out chunks left clear indications of the feasting done after he was dead. I *hoped*.

I felt miserable for him, imagining what he went through. I never would have thought I might, likely, die a similar way.

Statistic keepers say… what now are a person's odds of dying by gunshot or being eaten alive???

   "I'll take Fucked Up Odds for 600…"

90%, is the answer.

   "Death by zombie."

Please phrase that in the form of a question.

   "I apologize, Mr. Trebek. What is the chance of dying via zombie?

You are <u>absolutely</u> right.

The police later said he'd accidently shot himself in the gut.

I will never forget any detail of that moment—standing there while the scent made an imprint on my mind—like a sixth sense.
Since then—I can't eat meat on the bone.

I stopped eating store made burritos and fast food chicken sandwiches when more than once something crunched in them and I couldn't identify it.
Cartilage? Bone? Teeth?
Too close to the animal. No skin. No bone. And the only time I better see anything like bloody is in steak. I don't know why it's different. It just is.

So I just can't understand how I did that.

Will I have to do it again?

Would I be wise to do it, no matter what they do or what my instincts say? It's a matter, I think, of paying now… or later.

7:21pm

I've come to a decision. No more confrontations.

Run and hide will be a mantra. A way of life—literally.

I'm done with this shit.

Here's a question I never asked myself:

Would I rather go through the apocalypse as the weak, guilt ridden person I was before

-or-

as a stranger that does *whatever* she has to do to live? Anything she has to do.

I don't like to take chances.
And that's always included strangers.

I need to be someone I can live with, because that's the home where my thoughts live and rest and breed.

I need to talk to God—on my knees, with my hands palm to palm, thumbs together against my chin—like I was taught, when I was little.

I need to get this out more than just on paper.

I'm sorry.

Dec 17 10:59am

I wish I didn't have to travel by road, but my attempts to negotiate woods and even fields have been futile with the supply wagon (suitcase) I'm pulling.
In keeping with my early New Year's Resolution, I'm learning to run and be happy about it.

I improvised a leash for Mr. Ages and almost had to drag him half a mile to get away from twenty-some busy bodies that were loitering on the freeway.

I didn't see them, only three were on my side of the enormous accident piled across most of the four lanes.

I can handle three—not dozens.

I was glad for the suitcase's wheels, such as they are. Not exactly muddin' tires.

I would have lost *a lot* if I'd had to leave it.

I wish I could leave the ice behind.

Unless I get away from this area, I know it will be with me until spring.

Dec 18 6:09am

I'm going to save one of my Chocolate Royale Slimfasts for that last meal of fruit cocktail. I really liked that.

SlimFast: Official sponsor of Survivors of the Zombie Apocalypse.

Do you know what you'd have for your last meal?

I'm sorry.

Most people would probably rather not think about it.

Dec 19 10:58pm

All but a few stray beams of the sun remained, since the horizon began its supper, each day a little earlier than the last.

Through a cloud of breath I saw a small cluster of vehicles left on the roadway. Through the strange light of dusk they looked like colossal black bison sleeping between snow drifts. A bare patch of pavement here, a foot and a half of snow there... all blanketing and polishing a treacherous layer of ice.

What, at first, appears to be four vehicles is actually a car and two trucks, one towing a collapsed Starcraft camper.

I stared them down, looking up more than once to survey the growing darkness. Between that and falling temperature, I felt cornered into making one of the four our home for the night.

The vehicles had been there for some time, I thought. I sensed they were a convoy. The hood of one truck was open—the game changer for these poor bastards, whatever went wrong there. We go through everything, starting first with the camper, because that, I decide, will be our motel.

It's fairly comfortable inside. The tiny, half door on one side, gives me a false sense of security and concealment, like we were in a burrow.

The other vehicles were too open—not safe to sleep in. Frankly, they looked colder too.

The camper was collapsed for travel, but it was shelter enough for us. In the cold, sleeping in cramped spaces is a delight. I just can't think about it too much, or I start to panic. In the dark, I pretend I'm outdoors. If I think about how little air is there, suddenly I feel like there's no air at all.

Mr. Ages <u>does</u> break wind several times every night and is the worst thing about the smaller space.

At least I can stretch out in here—I've been pretty close to a human pretzel some mornings.

I woke up to something trying the locked door.
I put both hands over Mr. Ages' mug. Though he's actually improved a lot. His growl was low and deep. I silently comforted him and prayed it wouldn't hear.
One bark and I was doomed.

I would never know if it was safe to come out.
Eventually, I'd have to take the chance... I hate that.

I heard the sound of multiple pairs of footsteps.

"I got some Planters!" someone exclaimed.
I clamped my hands harder. I sucked in on a breath of surprise.

Busy bodies are too busy to talk...

"How much?" a second man answered.
"About half a cup," the first man returned. "That locked?"
"Yep."
"Probably everything's in the back of the pickup."
"It's been picked to pieces."

I hoped they wouldn't realize how recently.

I checked my watch. 9:21pm—it was still dark out, so I hoped
I'd lucked out and all the evidence of "me" would be obscured
in shadows.

I also prayed that Mr. Ages and I had walked around enough
that they wouldn't know where we ended up.

How could I run and hide?

"I need to piss," someone announced.
I heard two "shhh's".
But it was the second man who ordered: "Keep it down! You
want to draw in every zombie in a hundred miles?"
The third man said something. He sounded irritated.
"It *is* a big deal!" the first man countered.
"You make it sound like I'm trying to get us killed—you're the
one who—"

Then all of them were yelling. The second man, I heard say
something about making a mistake. The first man said "—
always doing stupid stuff—" I don't know who they were
talking to.

"Hey! He's got something!" I heard a woman exclaim.
"Goddamn it—I told you about concealing food!" the first man said
"It's not!"
"Show me!"
Then I heard fighting.

A weight struck the side of the camper.
I heard punching—someone was pushed or shoved. I heard the woman scream. It was loud enough, I think, that no one heard Mr. Ages get out a bark. I closed his face into my armpit and folded myself around him. We lay like fetal twins, listening hard and hearts racing.

"What are you doing?" one of the men cried out in a voice so distorted with panic I couldn't tell if I'd heard his voice already. The woman screamed again. There was a cry of pain.
It sounded like right over my head, someone uttered, "Oh God..."
"Let's go!"
The woman refused.

"Fuck you then!" I imagined the words screamed right against the side of her head.
"Wayne!" she cried.
"They're gonna get cha."
"Wayne!" she wailed.
Then she made an identical sound, but without the shape of a word.
"Look at all this shit he has on him!"
"Piece of shit!"

I heard male groans and cries to every "thwack!"
"We gotta go!" a man said urgently.

I heard something thump and slide along the opposite side of the camper.
I heard running. More screaming.

And then I heard things, taking their time crossing the crunchy, snowy ground.

It's been about twenty minutes, since whoever was left behind finally died, the beaten man, and probably the woman too.

There will be two more busy bodies now.

I've released my WWE hold on Mr. Ages' head.
Mr. Ages looks worried. His ears are laying out flat. His "eyebrows" are pinched.

When I pet him, he leans into the cup of my hand, but mostly, I know, he wants to see what I'm going to do about this. And I feel like he wants to know what's expected of him.
I know some people think projecting "human" qualities on animals is stupid.

Can someone be so ignorant to think that humankind has a monopoly on emotions and thoughts?

But then, it wasn't that long ago since popular opinion was that black people were animals, were dumb and had no feelings too.

I don't know why anything people ever did should have surprised me.

Why race and ethnicity were terms too hard for people to understand—
—anyway. I was just thinking about ignorance. Which is a lot easier to think about than the pressing issue.

Do the dead know I'm here? Will they leave?

And if the answers to each, in that order are: Yes and No—
Then how do I get out of this?

In a Starcraft, in a possible lose/lose situation, I can't help but
think: What would Isaac Clarke do?

Dec 20 3:32pm

It's freezing.

Mr. Ages has been making miserable sounds—he needs to get
out and "go."

I can't tell if what I think I'm hearing is real or not.
I can't tell if they're out there, but I need to decide before
nightfall.

It's getting too late, right now, because I'm not going to crawl
out the door and find shelter nearby.

I have a pretty good flashlight, headlamp and lantern, but
what's light is light. What's dark is dark. More than once I've
swung the light and found busy bodies where they weren't a
moment before.

I wish I knew what I'm hearing.

I don't know if what I'm hearing is real.

I thought I heard Marie laughing out there.
I thought I heard growling.
I thought I heard clinking nails.
I thought I heard something on the roof.
I thought I heard breathing against the door.

I thought I heard my mother crying. I know the sound of it like I know the smell of death and react to both about the same. But this time, I thought I heard Marie. The sobs turned to laughter.

Maybe I was dreaming.

I'm sure I was.

Obviously, I had to be.

I can't make him hold it anymore.

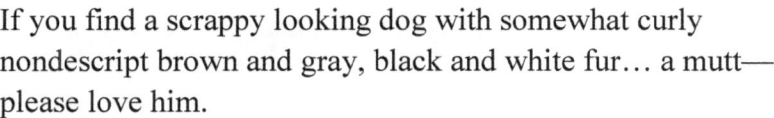

I hope this isn't the last I'll write.

If you find a scrappy looking dog with somewhat curly nondescript brown and gray, black and white fur… a mutt— please love him.

I do.

Christmas Eve 11:43am

I'm wondering what other people are doing.
How many people even know the day?
If they do, are they celebrating? Mourning? Cursing?

This is a day a lot of dreams and wishes teeter on becoming reality.
Add to them my wishes and prayers for all of us.

Tomorrow I'm going to take a personal day.

Merry Christmas.

Dec 26 5:04am

Do you want me to write even if I have nothing to say?

I guess I can say this—I'm still in Illinois... unless I'm *back* in Illinois, then I would have been in Indiana.

Anyway, I know where I am.

I wish I could make my mind stay with me. Or, if it has to go, I wish it would only leave me when my body is safe. And when it takes me with it, I wish, just once, it would take me to places in my mind not so closely resembling Hell.

Dec 27 8:29am

Have been thinking a lot about what happened at the Starcraft. Loneliness can be hard and I don't even have real loneliness, but how could someone give up all the benefits of being alone to take the chance of that shit happening to them?

I would think a person would be safe with people they knew before this started—but did any of us know who we *really* were before?

Does anyone *really* know themself before they face catastrophe? Can you know who you are before you're confronted with a situation demanding another kind of person?

How many "strong" people back down?
How many "weaklings" step up?

How much worse is this than it had to be, because someone puts their needs, their life, before others' when it didn't have to be "me or them"?

I saw another parent leave her own child—who had some way to go yet, running to the car. The selfish bitch didn't look back, not once. The child, no more than four or five, was overcome by the dead. In my mind is the image of that little frightened face shining with tears. I can still hear her screams, where they mingle with too many others'.

My mom would have left me too.

I saw people run from their overrun homes to a neighbor's, only to be turned away or blown away. Then I later saw them wandering around hungrily, with those horrific, ungodly eyes.

Way to be, looking out for #1!

I'm guilty of that.

I killed those men. I killed that lady who attacked me for attacking people she knew. Loyalty is a virtue beyond many others, these days. And I killed her for it.

To love someone is a privilege.

How horrible was it for her to see me spring on the rifleman? If she cared about him—it had to be somewhere in the spectrum of fear and desperation and proactive grief everyone felt when it happened to them.

Jan 2 4:49pm

I ran out of ink.
Once it warmed inside my shirt, I got this new pen working. I always kept the other one clipped on the middle of my bra to keep it warm and working.
I'm glad it worked.

I have a couple pencils now and the rest of the pens from this pack.

So far I'm not seeing any form of winter that I think I can survive in the long term.
That's what I want.

I want to have a house again—a home—a place that I can take care of—will also take care of me.

My shoes have almost had it.
I haven't had any luck finding replacements. Nothing suitable anyway. Finding good walking shoes that aren't already worn down or are the right size has turned out to be a challenge.
I'm too scared to go into town.

As far as foraging goes, mostly, I've been counting on cars and homes that don't look too big and don't appear to be occupied.
I also count on gas stations, like this one, that are a little off the beaten path.

There's not much here, but it had the two things I really wanted: shelter and a pen.

The first thing I look for, when I can no longer get around investigating a house *now*, are if the windows are covered: this could indicate it being occupied by someone else.

No one would leave their windows uncovered—at least not this long into it, would they?
I watch for hints of light.
I look for activity in the yard and listen around the house.
The last bit I leave to Mr. Ages' good judgment. And it is good.
But I've never found a house with a living person.

-

I'm hoping that I've heard the end of unnecessary barking. I think he gets it now. At the house, there was no reason to be as strict as I am out here, so he wasn't learning anything then.

There *were* busy bodies outside when we left the camper.

That afternoon his barking saved my life.

Seneca advised, "Choose as a guide one whom you admire more when you see him act than when you hear him speak."

I don't know if it was because he had to go so bad, but as soon as I turned the knob enough that the door was loose, he pushed through. The small half-door slammed loudly against the exterior of the camper.

Outside, I heard Mr. Ages barking like crazy.
I went out feet first with the hammer ready.
I pulled out the suitcase with my free hand.
A corpse moved right past me, brushing my head as it cleared the small entrance.
The skin prickled across my scalp.

He kept barking and kept them out of reach. His bark was different—defiant. His bark kept them fixed.
I went around the back of the camper, out of sight, and broke into a run as soon as I reached the shoulder—or I would have broken my neck on the ice.
I called him.

It took several times before he bolted to catch up, with a knob of poo sticking out of his ass.

For his sake, I wasn't going to mention this, because I am so proud of him, but the moment that keeps returning to the forefront of my thoughts is when he wiped out on the ice just as he reached me. Even as he hit the road on his side, his legs were still moving so fast.

I think it's at the forefront because I can't stop thinking about what might have happened if the spill had happened closer to *them*.

-

This illness is really starting to worry me. The fever is unrelenting. Worse than that is the crippling pain. I hate to straighten my left arm, so I fold it up like a chicken wing and hook my thumb in the strap of my pack to support the position. The afflicted area is too great to know where the problem's derived from. My left lung hurts when I draw a breath—or maybe it's the meat around it. My back and ribs hurt. My arm is almost useless. My shoulder is a full of heat and angry white spots fill my eyes when anything touches it… so I am really, really afraid that the worst has come from the stabbing.

It was driven almost to the hilt, but I can't remember how big it was—I only remember throwing it away. I never regarded the wound as insignificant, but I would feel foolish to die from it— I don't know why… or maybe can't articulate it.

Jan 3 7:37am

If I had nothing to worry about, I'd wish there was a man here today. Someone strong, who'd do some of the worrying for me. Someone who'd protect me.

I want to know what it feels like to fall asleep in someone's arms and waking up still in them.

I'd like to know what kind of woman I would be to him...
Would I be a bitch? A nag? Dominating? Supportive? Loving? Submissive?
I want to know.

Things I felt in relationships, when I was young, weren't love. They weren't even lust.

I didn't understand real desire until I was just about to turn twenty. Then I had a whole different part of my mind to get to know. A different part of my being came alive.

I think I was close to having everything I'd ever want, then.

I want to know how well I can love someone.
I want a second chance.

It's that simple.
Today.
Tomorrow it might just be lust.
The next day I'll probably be glad to be alone.

Then there's no one to leave you. And no one else's feelings or future to consider when you're dying.

What am I going to do without you?

What's going to happen if I die...?

Being alone or being with someone, the question is: Who wants to be hurt?

Jan 4 10:10am

I woke up in a house. I don't know how I got here. I'm not sure where I am. I don't think I've lost any supplies. The "essentials" in my pack are still intact. I'm mostly wearing my glasses now. My contact solution is almost gone.

I'm not wearing my glasses. They are folded up the on a mission style end table, on top of a bass fishing magazine.

After I collect my things, and my thoughts, I realize I am shaking, violently. I woke up with tears on my face, which isn't exactly news anymore. The shaking—that bothers me.

I wring my hands, they hurt. They are sore and cold. They are cramped from the fists they make to move the trolley suitcase. From the fists I make around my weapons. The fists I make in my pockets, to keep them warm. The fists I make against the arm of the couch when I sit up.

Can't take this. Can't take this.

Have to.

Do I?

I dreamt I was dead... God asked me, "Isn't this what you wanted?"

How would you feel if you made a wish that destroyed the human race? What would you do if they came back for revenge?

I just feel sick.

I'm afraid to die.

Jan 5 3:04pm

I think people writing their will, their last wishes, their final farewells must have felt like I feel writing this journal.

I don't want to be like the woman next door.

Trying to capture whatever matters about me and record what is happening makes me feel like a person who knows they're dying and needs to get their life down so their grandkids will know how they lived—who they were and in that way, explaining more about who *they are*.

Am I writing to someone who will turn out to be no one? It makes me feel like I've been "Catfished" by God.

Why would I have felt such a strong compulsion to write if God knew that mine would be the only eyes to ever see it? Statistically speaking, the number of lives left for God to monitor has dropped exponentially. I may be the only living tenant in His supervision.

Wow. That's actually a little intimidating.

It almost felt like the air pressure changed.

There was definitely a sense of being lost to God before—most of us spend so much time trying to find Him.

Back then, all our little or great moral indiscretions were comparable to the acts of billions of other people.

Back then, a person could tell themselves they're a better person than they are because of all the "worse people".
We are not being graded on a curve. I feel the teacher's eyes on me. The only person in detention.

I suddenly have this feeling, in almost absolute certainty, that the NEED to start filling this journal is like God taking a paper and pen and saying, "I need a written confession."
Only *almost* absolutely certain—because I believe that *you* are out there—or will someday be.

Maybe I'll try to write a confession. It might be good for me. Even so, there are things I've felt and done and known that I have to deny to myself that even God knows.
The unspeakable.

Things too ugly for the light of day.

I've always been gullible—but now it seems *I* can talk myself into anything too.

Mr. Ages is <u>watching</u> me.
Is he watching me?
I'm probably projecting again—but his eyes look so smart.
They look like he knows what I'm feeling and thinking.
Even what I'm writing.

I have a sense that I've known him for a lot longer than I have. He looks at me like he knows me. As if he always has. ~~It reminds me of the way my boyfrie~~

I'm giving myself goosebumps—I'm just projecting on him whatever way my mind needs to feel less lonely—whatever it needs to keep a firm hold in there—while I am sometimes so afraid my mind is getting lost—I hope I never write to you when I'm like that.

I hallucinate. I sometimes can't tell what's dream.
~~And when my thoughts start going place—looking for people.~~

179

I'm freaking myself out for nothing.

I just asked Mr. Ages if he was a dog or if, for authenticity, God would appreciate his apocalyptic spy to eating so much shit? God forbid we should pass the droppings of deer or rabbits...

4:16pm

I've been thinking... and I don't think I can write a confession. So I'll just start by listing some regrets.

4:52pm

Next to the journal are three sheets of paper I tore out of the back. I read and reread what I wrote. I read and reread my regrets. I read and reread a list that might look something like what Saint Peter will hold against me.

I don't remember being so emotionally fragile, but I feel like I'm crying all the time. Being sick, feeling vulnerable never helps... I suppose stress has a lot to do with it—I can maybe blame lack of sleep, but... I feel like I'm falling apart.

Why did I think that would do me any good?

What is the point of feeling regret when half the time you can't do anything about it and the other half of the time you don't because it would be too horrible for you to try?

What is the point of a lot of the things we feel?

Sometimes people ask themselves "What's the point?" too much.

We have to know, eventually, we will reach a conclusion.

How many people like what they discover?

Outside, Nature is quietly reclaiming what is rightly hers. For most people there was an unspoken or completely unconsidered "understanding" about people and nature coexisting. I think there were people who assumed she'd one day fight back.

Again, maybe the most important or insignificant question:

Is this nature fighting back?

And/or is this something we did to ourselves?

Jan 6 9:01am

I'm wearing out my photographs.

I'm guessing it's a combination of climate and dirty hands, but they're really beat up.
I'm afraid of losing the faces and the moments.

Are any of them left?

I feel as if their images keep them around, somehow. That they're really alive someplace else, right now. But if the pictures are gone, if I ruin them—it's like *they* are erased and yet I can't stop looking.

I stare at them until my eyes burn.
Who else will remember their faces?
And I need to remember...
Remember when this? Remember when that?

I feel like I could forget myself.

I don't want to think of anybody as winking out, like the woman that was eaten by Neighborhood Watch back in Rhinelander.

I dream of dying like *her*—not how I've seen *anyone else* die. It's always the way she died.

I can hardly remember what her face looked like when it wasn't screaming. I didn't see her many times.

There was the first time, when I realized there was someone at that house. I was kneeling in the yard, to steady myself as I tried to coax a sliver to the surface of my right palm. The corner of my left eye caught a faintest movement. Then from the unchanging face of the house across the street, a dark rectangle seemed to peel back like a sardine lid. A living person emerged, just enough to do what she had to. She'd thrown out a mixing bowl of, what I assumed to be, piss. She used the back of her wrist to push the long, rippling red hair off her cheek. I think it might have touched her nose or mouth, in ticklish, intolerable way.

She slipped back inside and for the next few days, at least when I was watching, it was like she never was.

Intermittently, I saw evidence she hadn't left. Most the time they were only fleeting glimpses or just the disturbance of a curtain or blinds that told me where she was.

She reminded me of Bette Midler in *Outrageous Fortune*. Her hair, build and basic theme of her attire was remarkably close, however outdated.

But I can hardly remember her face.

Jan 7 4:13pm

I wanted to find a library, but thank God I won't have to take any chances in a town, not for a book—because I found what I needed right here. A book about climate and stuff in the US.

Kentucky, Tennessee, Missouri, maybe Kansas would suit me.

I guess when I find the place I'll know.
I'm deep in the stomach of winter.

I'll be some time in the climate I fear the most.

It does slow them down, the winter. The cold.

It slows us all down.

Jan 8 9:40am

Am staying another day here. A winter storm came up last night—howling and blowing snow. To be out in it would be suicide.

The wind-chill is merciless.

Merciless… the word seems so appropriate. But I have to kind of laugh at that when I think of winters in Rhinelander—which were better than the winters I knew in northern Michigan, where I lived until I was seventeen. It was nothing for winter temperatures to reach a -40 or -50 wind-chill to only soar to the high nineties in the summer. That's almost a 150 degree temperature change in less than a year. They are pretty tough stock in the Northern Midwest. I'm proud of that, even if I wouldn't even try a winter up there now.

I listen to Mr. Ages' nails as he paces, listening to the wind…

I wonder if he is answering it… Mr. Ages is making the weirdest sounds.

The last blast made the whole building rattle and groan. Mr. Ages answered with a sound like "Row" or "Whoa". His mouth is pushed out, short and puffy. I don't understand where all the mouth goes when dogs do that. Like how the bones in their face appear to slide into their skulls when they bare their teeth and their mugs get all short and wrinkled…

I said, "Oh?" back at him and he kinda rolled his head at me while cocking it. I dunno if he feels mocked, but he was.

A series of almost verbal sounds followed. He looked like he was pleading his case. Seeking understanding. I told him, "I know" and tried to comfort him.

He's never acted like this. Maybe there's something out there I don't know about. A wendigo, perhaps? An ice wraith? The Horseman of Death? A banshee? A squirrel?

I'm trying to be in a relaxed state of mind because every sound sounds like <u>something.</u> I don't feel like I should be afraid all the time… tense all the time anymore. Jumping at shadows… scrambling to check every bump, thump, scratch and skitter. I don't know how I'm going to sleep tonight!

I suppose it's just as well, because I haven't been sleeping that good anyhow.

It's always too cold, even with a sleeping bag. My arms and shoulder aren't healing right or maybe at all.

I know the infection is bad.

I took five aspirin and was finally able to put medicine on them. I could only do a half-assed job on whatever was going on in my shoulder, since the wound isn't exactly accessible to treat or even see what's going on. There was about 1/2 a tube of Polysporin in the medicine cabinet, in addition to a lot of things I had no use for—dentures, estrogen, hot oil, those nasty floss sticks and several prescriptions that I didn't understand. But I did understand one of them:

Valium.

I stared at it for probably a minute and a half.

I felt like it was there, waiting for a *quitter*.

I didn't mean to, but when I closed the cabinet I did it hard enough that the sound actually startled me and everything fell over inside. My heart was pounding.
When I took hold of the cabinet door and slammed it again and again and again, I meant to. Only when the glass shattered did I think about why. I stared at the flattened globs of gilded glue, that once held the mirror to the cabinet face. Even while pieces of it littered the counter, sink and floor, I still expected to see myself. I felt accusations fly at the reflection I didn't find and hated myself for considering, for even a moment, what I had let pass through my mind…

I'm no fucking quitter.

Who the fuck could waste their life so ungratefully, especially after so many people didn't have any fucking choice what their last hour would be???

Lots of people.

If you don't already know it.

Lots of fucking people.

Nobody wants to go through this.

Well, that's probably not true.

After all, I did.

Jan 9 5:39am

The weather's not letting up at all.

I took Mr. Ages out and the wind ripped my breath away.
The snow and savage gusts have scattered dead branches
across the yard. Trees make sounds like firecrackers when they
fall. A huge old tree in the next yard came crashing down when
we were out there. My heart flew into my throat. Mr. Ages ran
to get back inside. He stomped and wriggled urgently in front
of the closed door, imploring me. He tries to keep all his feet
off the ground at the same time.
What's there to be afraid of?

Everything, there is to be afraid of. We are afraid of
everything. Together he and I are cowards, so we can brave
this nightmare.

Sometimes I forget, or take for granted, the fear in him,
because he doesn't always show it. I'm not as frightened as he
is by the felled tree. It just startled me a little. When I realized
what it was, I just had to calm down my physical being. It's
like a rattling old vehicle, unsteady and jittery all the time. My
nerves are fucked. I shudder all the time, like I'm going to stall.
But my consciousness feels better.

It's my turn to comfort him.

We're going to be okay, I find myself thinking, so I make sure to tell Mr. Ages too. I think he believed me, once I let him back in.

I have a winter coat now and boots. They're a little tight, but they don't let snow in.

I'll live.

I'll live.

I'll live. I'll live. I'll live. I'll live. I'll live. I'll live. I'll live. I'll live. I'll live. I'll live. I'll live. I'll live. I'll live. I'll live. I'll live. I'll live.

I'll run and hide.

Jan 10 NOON

It sucks outside.

None of the food here is edible.

Even though I have supplies left, I can't stay—not unless I had gained supplies.
I don't want to be trapped.

Mr. Ages goes along with my choices.
I wonder if he ever doubts me.

Tomorrow we head out, no matter what.

Jan 16 2:49pm

This morning I woke up to voices. They weren't in my head.

Someone said, "I think she's coming around."
"Just be ready for anything," they were saying.

My vision was blurry at first, but my sense of smell was working fine. I smelled campfire—no, it was charcoal. I could hear something sizzling.

I tried to sit up and two large hands closed on my shoulders, both helping me and slowing me down. He smiled hugely and hollered over his shoulder—"Yah, she's awake."

I was a little alarmed that he should be so loud, but didn't have the strength to even show it, even though I was sure it would draw the attention of the dead.
He asked if I was hurt.
I shook my head.
I didn't think so.

"Think you can eat something?"
I asked for something to drink first.
Then I got a chance to look around.

There were three males and four females of different ages.
There was an improvised clothes line.
There was a lot of camping gear—some of it I thought was
mine. In fact, I am sure was.

A young man squatted in front of a little Weber grill. He said,
"You can have a beer if you don't mind it warm."

Beer?
"Yeah," I agreed.

It was colder than he gave it credit for, but did nothing for my
thirst.

"This might seem quick, but we are mostly on the go, so I'm
going to be blunt. If you feel like it, you can come with us in
the morning," said the cook. He turned over a hunk of red
meat, revealing beautiful brown and black, sizzling grill marks.

"With you?"

The cook forgot the cooking for a second and turned mostly
toward me—his eyes were deep and penetrating dark blue.
Like a night without stars. Eternally deep—easily drowned in. I
loved him, instantly. I felt like crying.

"You're gonna be okay—I promise. You'll be with us."

Promise?

"Promise?" I croaked.

"Yeah—as long as you promise not to hurt anyone."

"Okay," I said dumbly—90% of my attention was on the beer.

The guy had let go of my shoulders and went to retie the clothes line higher or tauter.

The woman, standing near it, leaned in—I couldn't hear her, but her lips asked, "Is she okay?"
The man shrugged, but said, "Sure."

I heard heat bugs, cicadas whirring. It seemed like it would be warm, but wasn't. It was cold, in fact. My fingertips were numb. I felt like I was missing something. Panic mounted, my eyes scoured the scattered parts of me—the headlamp hanging there, my bag propped up near me, this and that I knew were mine divided throughout the camp. Something more important than anything I saw was gone, but I had no idea what it was.

A woman my age cast me an earnest, reassuring smile.

"What is that?" I asked the cook. I didn't want to look a gift horse in the mouth—but I worried that was exactly what it could be.

"Beef," he said nonchalantly, jabbing his tong at "somewhere" over his shoulder. "There's a pasture over there."

It was suddenly later, not just in the day, but the seasons. The sun swung dizzyingly, and heavily to the other side of the sky. I felt like what was gone could never be found, but was washed with a feeling of indifference. A disregard completely contrary to a deeply buried part of me.

"Would you like some coffee?" a lady asked.

"Man in the bathroom?" I said absently.

"That's right," she laughed. It was contagious.

I kinda knew it would be.

The group laughed, with all the flat emotionlessness of cardboard. I opened my mouth. The motion of and expression of laughing came out without sound.

Then it was nightfall, I had eaten and felt truly welcome—they talked to me like we were old friends.

It finally registered that it was summer. It was summer again.

My watch was dead.

I'd lost months!

I asked what happened to me, if they knew. They looked confused. The cook raised his alluring blue eyes to me and answered:

"What happened to all of us?"

That's when I heard screams. My heart shot up my throat like vomit. I felt like I was choking on the smooth meat of the organ.

I shook too hard to hold my hammer without dropping it.

What's wrong with me? What's WRONG with me?!

I looked to the group for answers. They were staring at me.

I̲ was screaming.

I *was* screaming.

I sat up fast and slammed my head into the ceiling of the truck—though I wouldn't realize I'd done that until later, when my head hurt and I found the bump. At that moment, all I knew was that I was driven out of sleep by pain and my own screams.

I was drenched in a cold sweat. I felt flu-ish and frightened—and threatened. I was crying and I clamped both hands over my open mouth. The scream poured through my fingers like I'd tried to block water from the tap with a fork.

I think I smell her perfume.

My left hand fell away and I bit hard on the flesh between my thumb and first finger.

All of them… They were people I know are dead.

Jan 17 11:01am

I am in love with the smell of fryer oil.

I remember stepping outside and that smell hitting me—the "fair food" smell. It goes beyond nostalgic.

Food of the gods—I definitely associate it with a multifaceted desire from my childhood. Less than once a year—maybe—I would get to have something from one of those glass-faced food castles.
I felt like everyone else went there every week.

It lost the grandeur and mysticism when I grew up and found out that some people eat almost every meal there and there are some people who never knew the inside of any fast food place and didn't care.

As a child I was a prisoner of the word "normal"—which never means the same thing twice.

-

This diner's dingy.

It's dingy in a way that suggests it wasn't all that clean even before this happened. It has only been seven months, or so. For now, I still see the ghosts of the way things were.

For example, if I go into a house that has been picked clean, turned over, ripped to pieces, windows smashed, doors kicked in—I can still find ghosts of the lives that inhabited it. They might manifest sassy or loving remarks left on notes on the fridge or dry-erase board. I see furniture, still original from the owner. The décor. I see the way clothes are arranged in the master bedroom—are there "his" and "hers" sides?—are they mixed up?—what is on their respective nightstands. Are there hot oils in their bathroom? Are there ball-gags and whips in the shoebox under the bed?

Here, the ghosts say there was a waitress who was a pretty friendly person. The order slips waiting on a line between the counter and the kitchen have distinctly different writing on them—one of the waiters or waitresses puts "smiley faces" on the orders. Like on the order for a deluxe burger that says, "No meat". Then a smiley face.

The same smiley face is on the schedule on the back where a couple notes were up asking to give away shifts:
"Sure" or "I can cover it" …and the smiley face.

They were hiring. There are resumes on the manager's desk.

She has a husband who's balding and had a huge handlebar mustache. They have a son who got a little too much of his dad's nose and his mom's chin. They look happy. It makes me think the employees were treated well here, which means the customers were probably treated well.

That might be why it's dingy. Maybe they didn't take a little built up grease that seriously. No draconian task master. No sociopathic tyrant.

I'm sitting on the reddish-orange, by the square foot, tile behind the counter.

I'm in my sleeping bag. It's never zipped up.
We're not taking stupid chances.

I got a sweater on Mr. Ages. I think it's from the last place we stayed. I put a long-john shirt on him for pants. I'll spare the description of how I mutilated it to make it work in that capacity, but trust me, it does. It doesn't seem to bother him too much.

I found a car with almost a full tank of gas, but couldn't get it to turn over.
"Fuck you" didn't cover that one.

I feel, now, that I've been cold all my life. I had looked forward to a heated car—and making some time.

I feel like my time wasted and miles lost are like the National Debt.

So tonight I'm thinking through movies I wish I could watch for real. I don't have any trouble remembering my favorites, because I over watched those. There are some I wish I'd watched again, but, no matter how good, were too hard to imagine watching through a second time. Like *Grave of the Fireflies, Tae Guk Gi,* and *The Vanishing.*

I have some videos on my iPod, but I can't use earbuds in this environment and I don't want to run down my battery. If the car had started I could have recharged it. The car was deader than the dead.

Yesterday, I was thinking of men—first celebrities, then people I thought were *so hot* when I was growing up. I laughed about a lot of those. Then I thought about the men who I regularly saw, in the life I had.

One was this guy who was a fireman or EMT or something, by the uniform he sometimes wore. He struck me as polite, at first.

The longer I knew him as nice, the more handsome he became.

I saw him at work pretty regularly—but he'd only been there twice and he bothered to remember my name. When you're used to indifference or rudeness that means a lot.

If what I experienced was the norm, about 85% of humanity was selfish, apathetic and rude.
I don't believe that was the norm.
Do I think he was an exception?

Sincerely, yes.

Jan 18 11:54pm

I've left that dingy stray trucker diner, Deb's Drive-Inn, this morning and am forced to stay in a car tonight. It's a lot more exposed than I'd ever choose—if I had another choice.

Mr. Ages will have to learn to fly soon because he can't keep his feet in the snow any longer and I am exhausted.

The cold <u>definitely</u> slows them down.

I saw one who was reaching out, but still as a statue.

I am 95% sure that I could have stood right in front of him and he could have done nothing—or nothing fast enough to matter.

Have you ever seen *Stir of Echoes*?

He reminded me of when the ghost touches Kevin Bacon and he gets all stiff and cold, reaching out.

It's not the first time I've felt bad for them, but I didn't think I could kill him, even though, for the first time I felt like it was just as good for him as it was for me.

If someone happened to be watching, would they just shake their heads or would they want to kill the woman they found sobbing over their mortal enemy? I don't know what to think of how I feel. Can I survive if my horror wanes? Will I be less cautious? Will I maybe make fewer nervous mistakes?

Can I just look at them like people that were—that they have died and this is what happens when something dies? Can I look at them as rotting and mutilated things that have a strong behavioral problem?

Should I be amazed or horrified at how quickly we grow accustomed to the gore?

-

We might not be sleeping in a car if I hadn't wasted time appreciating that busy body's "life", the time I wasted dwelling and deliberating… thinking about all of *us*.

In them, we see eyes and faces and movement that resemble life, but do they think and feel or do they imitate and just <u>do</u> what they <u>do</u>?

When I know the answer, I'll be like them and will be able to tell it to no one.

They don't talk. But sometimes I think they think… and sometimes I think they hurt.

The ones that seem *empty* must be the more "perfect" of… well, whatever they are. More perfect zombies… whatever…

In shows, when they want to depict something as a perfect killer, emotion is the first thing that's taken away.

I have horrible dreams.
But on the bright side, I guess that means I reach deep sleep. Maybe that's not so good.

I think too much.

What do I think about?

I grew up in a loveless home with two selfish adults who hated each other.

It's funny how when you lose someone your feelings about them usually improve. It's like you feel so bad for them, that they are dead or hurt, that you can't hate them as much as you did or should.

I often think about the rare "every-so-often" when I thought my parents actually loved me. Most the time I know they wished I never was. They did very little, if anything, to hide it.

I think about what made them that way. I knew relatively nothing about my grandparents because we never had anything to do with them... few of my aunts or uncles did—because they were mean old bastards... all four of them. They raised angry, abusive kids who hated each other in turn. I do not miss the angry, drunken phone calls in the middle of the night. One parents or the other... sometimes both... screaming into the mouthpiece strings of profanities that make light of any I've heard since.

I would lay in my bed, comforting a matted, plush killer whale, and listen to it and think about this purposeless machine called family... Sometimes, I felt bad that both of them, obviously, never got what they wanted in life. Now they are likely dead.

What kind of life was that?

And I, the summation of that miserable existence...

I said "I love you" every time I talked to them.

They would say it back.
...
I still wonder why.

When I was a child, I meant LOVE and I hoped that evoking the word would provoke LOVE.

When I tried to reach them and couldn't and everything in the world was going to shit—I loved them and meant it. The idea of anything happening to them hurts my soul so bad I feel it in my bones—*deeper*—to that feeling in our gut that lies so deep it seems it must exist outside us. The place that is warm, with hope and joy, bright with inspiration and enthusiasm, and sometimes a dark vacuum of dread and desperation... Good God...The deaths I've seen—when I think of the things that could have happened to them...

If they died—how? By what? By who?

Did they love each other in the end, like people do when they first got married? Maybe in the eleventh hour, overcome with a sense of loss and guilt?

No.

They got married because they were pregnant with me.
I doubt if love was required.

Jan 22 1:06am

Came upon a fairly fresh busy body of a man under a small wooden country bridge. It shambled out like a flesh colored grasshopper, with a human head—quirky or twitchy, like an image filmed under a strobe light, but with all the black frames edited out.

It was horrifyingly thin and naked as the day it was born. It didn't have a jaw and its neck was broken so its chin was almost parallel with its back bone. Its frozen tongue flopped freely over its upper face like a short red horn.

Its tongue actually seemed really long.

The busy body pushed through the drifting snow almost casually—like some creepy creature that lived under the bridge that was actually perfectly harmless.

I felt like Alice.

Who's that trip-trapping over my bridge?!?

I was crossing the bridge when it reached the road behind me. Mr. Ages kept looking back, but he didn't even growl—only his hackles were raised around the neck of his sweater and the back of his head.

 It couldn't catch up—we were so cold I was just thinking about moving and moving and moving on.

There was an overturned car mangled on the opposite side of the stream. I guess that's why he looked that way—all twisted and mangled himself.
I looked back.

The peach grasshopper was making good time, considering the cold and how broken he looked. Behind him though, I saw others coming out. I imagined some of them were possibly his family—a woman and two children who didn't look like they'd been dead that long either, but there were several others too. Maybe these were responsible for "turning" the family. Or maybe the whole family died in the crash.

I guess I should have been happy to see that, clearly, there were other people alive not that long ago.

What I did have were mixed feelings. No one in this situation is going to feel anything else when meeting "other people".

I hurried—no matter how my feet were killing me—if I let them slow me down—they would kill me.

About 10 miles later we found a house that didn't look vandalized, occupied by busy bodies or looted.

There was a long deceased person there—had killed herself in bed—a shotgun lay against her rotted body.

About an hour later, when I was finally able to make myself, I drug the corpse outside and spent the next long while looking for shotgun shells. I eventually did find the ammo. So I had about 8 shots in the handgun, 4 in the rifle and 13 shotgun shells... and somewhere in the vast Everywhere Else there are countless dead and countless survivors who might be armed and hostile. I will, of course, assume they are.

Run and hide.
Why take the chance?
Don't you love your life enough to not take chances?

I got a few more canned and dry goods here.

I couldn't get their vehicle to start. There is another house just up the road with an SUV in the driveway. But this one bedroom, no attic, no basement house was easy to clear.
We had a good supper—our first since the house where we found the Slim Fast. After, Mr. Ages and I lay down on the couch and tried to be warm.

It's against my better judgment, but being so tired of being cold, I overburdened us with blankets and Mr. Ages fell asleep on my back after we fought with each other, on the small sofa, for a comfortable way to sleep.

The first thing I realized when I woke up was that it was still dark. The second thing was that I was <u>warm</u>—snug as a bug—the third thing was that Mr. Ages was growling right into my ear—I could feel his bared teeth against it. His hot breath felt damp against my skin. His breath stirred the errant hairs that strung across my ear…like the mechanics of a spider's web.

We weren't alone.

My arms were tucked under my chest like I was praying. My LED lantern was on the table on the other side of the sofa arm. I was afraid to move.

My bag was on the floor to my left—the handgun was accessible. The lantern wasn't far away. I had to get Mr. Ages off of me without making too much sound, but in what order to do the things I needed to?

And where was <u>it</u>?

I felt like a child hiding under their covers from the boogieman—it was <u>unthinkable</u> to have your arms or feet out of the blankets.
I was afraid to reach for either light *or* gun—I knew I'd feel teeth sink into me.

Right then, its only option to bite was my head.
Supposing it was a busy body…

I slowly straightened both my arms underneath me—I went from mummy, to chicken, to Transformer, to airplane.
I turned the dial of the lantern with one hand. The other hand's fingers, wrapped around the cold handle of the handgun.
It felt too cold outside the blankets.

As the gun came out and bluish white light came on, I was about to order Mr. Ages off me when I saw a busy body just about pass by the room.

The Grasshopper.

Its inverted legs, with outward facing feet, were stepping—two steps more and it would have been out of sight, but in mid-step it reversed so perfectly it looked like it was being rewound.

He looked right as me—his eyes seemed too small—they were wide set and lived far back in the eye socket, like his eyeballs themselves were shy and peeking out.

Mr. Ages snapped and snarled and dug his nails into me. My shoulder screamed. I *heard* the force of fluid drain from the infected wound.

He lunged off of me, struggling out of the blankets.

I felt a bite then, felt teeth clamp on me and squeeze through the layers of blankets to get at me. I kicked out. My foot, through blanket, connected with something and it fell.

Mr. Ages had the busy body, who was nearly on top of us, by the back of his shirt and was yanking him away.

Something bit my ham.

I rolled onto my back, without Mr. Ages' weight and shot it— the little boy.
The girl, who I'd kicked, was getting up.

I shot the one Mr. Ages was struggling with before I shot her.

Grasshopper was only two feet from my face then. He tried to reach for me, but had to keep dropping his hand to balance his broken body.

I wailed when I squeezed the trigger. How long it had been since blood was bright red and fluid enough yet to spatter? A huge dark whole erupted from Grasshopper's head. With a wooden thump, his grotesque form fell into a pile of itself, like legs giving out under a folding table.

Once I gathered myself together, I leapt up and called Mr. Ages to follow me.

We started in the hall that led to the bathroom and bedroom that made an "L" shape that reached the kitchen and front door—which was standing wide open. The other busy bodies were coming in.

I spent the last of my handgun rounds and came back with the hammer and screwdriver for the last two.

My first thought was: *There weren't that many under the bridge!*
That *I saw*, I guess.

What I angrily thought was—
      "THERE WERE <u>NOT</u> THAT MANY"
                      —like I was cheated.

The second thing I thought and then *did* was get the bodies out of sight of the road. I took them, one by one, around the side of the very small house. The somewhat bloody and quite fleshy trail looked more suspicious than the bodies would have, but it was too late to do anything to fix it.

My third thought zeroed in on the front door—how the hell did they get in?

I turned the doorknob—it <u>was</u> locked.
And I thought <u>that</u> defiantly too.
See! It wasn't <u>my</u> fault.

I closed the door. I stood back a second and pulled on it.
The door swung open.
I repeated the experiment, same results.

I closed it a third time and shoved on the door. I heard a "click"—I pulled the handle and it held fast.
"Mother fucker," I said.

I balled up the top blanket which had *something* like blood on it and put it in the hamper.

Stiffly, I went to the bathroom and took off my pants and checked my legs.

I felt pretty numb about it even though I was shaking. All the things I think were normal to feel were there, but the emotional traffic jam let nothing out but Polly Practical and she just wanted to check if the skin was broken.

No, but it was already bruising.

I can still feel it gnawing on me. Maybe I always will. I feel like those wind-up gag teeth that chatter had attacked my legs. It seemed like there was only teeth, even as the back of my mind protested that <u>it</u> had felt hands too. The Hands of Death. I imagined the teeth like dentures.

The one who bit me was the one I kicked—with teeth that never actually let up. They just relaxed and applied pressure, as if it was teething.

I was bruising—I could live with that.

Then I peed in the toilet—that felt like a reward. When I leaned forward, the skin drawing tight across my back, I felt the *sloosh* of pus, both watery and custardy, erupt from the puncture Mr. Ages made when pushing off of me. I took off my layers until I reached the last shirt, the one against my skin. More carefully I peeled this layer off, that I wouldn't spread the pus. I examined the discharge, a mixture of strawberry and cream, before folding the garment up and using it as a mitten while I squeezed around the puncture. As much as it hurt, it felt really good too.

I checked the shirt until mostly blood was coming out. By then I was nauseous from squeezing the wound.

I threw the shirt away.

I'd finished peeing some time earlier. I used the toilet paper and that was like a dream come true. But I discovered I'd got my period.

That explained a lot.

Those bastards followed me for miles. It's like I was saying before...

I took the rest of the blankets and lay down in front of the kitchen sink—the living room was too spoiled. Then we tried to sleep again.

The blankets must have muffled his senses enough so Mr. Ages hadn't noticed everything that happened while we were sleeping—or he was sleeping too hard; just like I was.

I folded a couple blankets underneath us and lay the sleeping bag down on top of that for a mattress. Then put all the remaining blankets on top of us again.

I thought the odds were in my favor to have no more visitors.

What *did* visit were nightmares.
That's why I'm awake and writing at this hour.

I'm glad I didn't have to write that <u>it</u> happened—the horrible (inevitable?) IT of being bitten and knowing the inevitable without any question marks around it.

Right now I'm thinking about what I'd write if that happened.

My first thought is that I'd hope Mr. Ages would know enough to stay away from me.

In this situation, as horrible as it would feel to do it—I think I'd kick him out and lock myself in—barricade the door so he might have a chance.

With absolute certainty, even if I died and came back as something that would kill him, I believe he would stay with me. ~~I don't think I could finish myself.~~

I thought about how long it would take to *happen*.

Would I have time to prepare Mr. Ages to be on his own? The only thing I know I'd have to do is put all my food supplies outside for him.

I can't stand the idea of being apart.

I think I'm done writing for today.

Jan 23 7:56 am

I just kept staring at the page.
The pen hovers and dives with intent to land and retreats.

Only one thought keeps repeating: "You were bitten."

I was bitten.

I think that I was strongly effected by what happened, but don't know to what degree yet.

Who wouldn't be disturbed by that? I'd say it's pretty natural that I should be effected. But my mind won't even let me peek at how much damage was done.

Sometimes I feel so close to losing it that it frightens me. All these nights of nonsensical, feverish dreams have led a greater part of me to believe I am closer to a complete breakdown than ever before. There is a small number on the picket line waving crudely made signs that plead for me to remember that I am sick. But it doesn't feel like a legitimate excuse.

I stop myself from tapping the pen on my knee, *again.*

I can't seem to make myself do anything.

Mr. Ages is clearly shaken.

We're moving on tomorrow. We need to.

Jan 24 1:06pm

When will the veil of surreal lift?
No matter how real the planning
No matter how real the ~~impossible~~ improbable.

Very often dreams feel every bit real until you wake.
Sometimes even for some time after.

I hope everyone I care about is alive—and well. To the standard "well" has become.

If they were anything less—I'd rather believe they were in Heaven.

If I was anything less than "well", could I stand to live?

I am no quitter.

Would I rather someone I loved died ~~or killed themself~~ if they were in a crappy situation now?

I would rather believe they were in Heaven than suffering.

Jan 25 4:39pm

I woke up with that piano version of *Bells for Her*, by Tori Amos, in my head. I love that song…

But a troubled mind is a place of distortion and my mind is taking this song the wrong way—in a very wrong way.
Just a few of the lines.
They won't quit repeating.

Devotion and resilience transform into fear and repulsion…and betrayal.

The lyrics have a double meaning now and make me aware of a most devastating horror I hope I never know.
Between illness, fear, love and death—I hear a death that becomes undeath.
She's describing exactly what many have seen…

But I dream it—I had a bad dream.

I had a horrible dream.

I'm so tired of nightmares—awake and sleeping.

Most people are victimized by people they know, right?

What if you *know* that a person would *never* hurt you—<u>ever</u>?

Then *this* happens and faces you love become *terrible*—people you love die and come back to kill you—to <u>eat</u> you and then you have to destroy flesh <u>you</u> would *never* have hurt.

Good God, that's miserable! Sympathy is too weak a word for what I feel for anyone who's known that.

It's bad enough dreaming it.

~~They were the people that~~

Dear God, if they are with you—tell them I love them.
But, if they *are* with you, I do not want to know until, by Your mercy, I am there to see for myself.

I do not ever want to see.
I do not <u>ever</u> want to see.

I would know God detested me if I ever had to face a version of them that

I know that face. I know that face. I know that face.
I love that face. That face loves me. I know. I know.
I know. I *know*.
So why is it making them be this way?
SHE WOULD *NEVER* HURT ME!
I know.
i know.

That face loves me.

Jan 26 9:18am

They said I "was missing out".
Where was the husband?
Where were the babies?

I would have them if I found the right someone, just like anyone else. Not just accept someone to fulfill a social checklist.

Now I wonder if it was fate, because I don't know what position I would be in—or who I could have lost.

Are you trying to make yourself feel better?

I think a lot about chance and fate.
And that a lot of good people who never find that *someone*.

There are a lot of bad marriages.
There are a lot of lonely people and a lot of people content to be single and abstinent.

I have never seen true romantic love.
We *wish* it for people we love.

To expect people to do what you perceive to be normal is ignorant.

I love her, but my one friend slept with more people than *she* could remember—sometimes even by the next morning.

As far as I'm concerned, she was no closer to reaching those "milestones"—unless she forgot her pill. However, I think that's too often a normal reaction after losing innocence and childhood—how do you become a stable adult when you were built without a foundation? When your sense of self and trust is ruined?

Still… why was I hounded more than her? Was it because they thought I *needed* the void of *him* filled?

I wouldn't have minded falling in love—even if nothing I've ever seen, collectively/historically, has ever made it look like anyone has ever found it to fall into.

Love almost resembles any other thing of myth or legend—like a genie's lamp, the Fountain of Youth, the meaning of life, or winning a Publisher's Clearing House Sweepstakes—each gives people something to dream about, but you don't have much evidence that its real—or, to give it some credit, *lasting*.

I believe in desire and loneliness. I think these are the forces that lose all the credit to "love" They are strong and universally understandable.

I think the absence of those forces was what was wrong between my parents and maybe many marriages.

Maybe I give too much power to the word, but I think a lot of people throw it around arbitrarily too.

I don't know where this rant came from. Just a little negative today. Holy shit.

Knowing what I know, how could I live with myself if I brought up a child in a family that even moderately resembled my own?

Can a family or marriage be perfect all the time?

No.

But why does it seem that the one quality which preserves relationships is tolerance? And that the social presence of "good couples", a lot of times, strikes me as pretending. Some instances, I know it is.

Have I envied what my married friends have?

Only when I'm horny.

Jan 27 2:10pm

I told my friends I was going to run away—leave Michigan for good. They said I wouldn't do it.

But when I was seventeen, I left.
I sometimes think this was about 16 years later than would have been good for me.

I didn't end up in Rhinelander right then, but within the year.
Some of my friends were mad at me.
It hurt them.

They felt abandoned.
But they knew I was hurting too.
It didn't take long before we were okay. But honestly, with how well we knew each other, I was surprised some of them held it against me as long as they did.

I'm still surprised some of them hadn't run away before I did.

My parents told me not to bother coming home.
I didn't intend to.

But eventually I wrote, until I felt I could call.
I felt I had to do these things—they were family.

I didn't want a relationship with them. But I felt obligated. I felt like I could never really let them go. Maybe it's because I really believed they wouldn't have any trouble letting go of me. I don't believe in throwing people away. But it's hard when people hurt you and you know you're not wanted—when its family. I also know I felt guilty "abandoning" them. I knew that, once I left, they were completely alone. They didn't have anything to do with any other people up there, either.

So I called them. And I said, like I said, "I love yous" that meant only "we're never totally severed."

After working on a dairy farm—*where they also kept chickens*—I answered an ad to be a roommate with a man who I ended up involved with. Our relationship was born out of our dysfunctional families, loneliness, necessity and understanding.

I loved his back and shoulders. I'd crawl up behind him and sink against them when we talked about important things. My favorite kind of talks.

Jan 28 9:48am

My neighbor's house was nearest when I found the hunter's
body. I told them. They called the police.
I never told my parents.
When friends asked, I admitted that I had found him.

I never talked about it again.
And no one asked.

Feb 1 3:27am

I want ~~that~~ a Dr. Pepper.

Feb 2 1:58pm

I had no expenses on the farm and saved enough to finally
move out, feeling I'd taken advantage of their kindnesses
enough. The missus offered to let me take her car off her hands
for a song and a dance. I looked it up on blue book and made
them a fair offer.

I talked to the guy who placed the ad a couple times over the
phone before I drove over to look at the house.

For lack of a better description, the yard looked "quietly" kept.
The North and South of that being Jungleland and Sickeningly
Immaculate. The house was like any other mid-west
townhouse. It was yellow with white trim. Ranch style. There
was a dense growth of lilies around the sides of the house and
huge cedar bushes—the growth of either spoke of an earlier
owner—the guy I talked to on the phone was in college and
had to be younger than any of these plants.

When he answered the door, my first thought was that it wasn't going to work out. He turned out to be a little older than me, but all I knew at the time was that he was young.

I thought two things: He's going to drive me crazy with insane college buddies... and I was insecure with how handsome he was.

When a person comes home they should be able to let their hair down, wear ugly clothes and be themselves.

I thought I'd have to stop somewhere on the way home from work to get ready for going home.

Moving away from the front door to show me around, I got my first look at the back I would someday know by heart. At the time, it wasn't that sentimental—and the way I admired him wasn't at all sensitive. I was eighteen and I'd been slapped in the face by a mature sense of attraction.

He kept house much the same way as he kept the yard—there were no illusions about him keeping things spotless—and he hadn't spazzed out a thirty minute touch up of a trashed house to impress me.

He had a calming and even voice—he was very casual—like I was a friend of a friend he was putting up. Little by little, as he showed me around, I drank up his comforting energy and rather than being insecure about it, let myself enjoy when he entered my personal space to show me this or that. I savored the warmth and fragrance of him when his body brushed against mine, reaching past me to point out something he wanted to replace.

His last two roommates had graduated in May—he said he had been comfortable with the expense of being by himself over the summer—I assumed that was his way of telling me he wasn't going to be a flake with the rent.

Then, for the first time, he looked me right in the eyes. He told me he hoped to get by with just one roommate.

His eyes were intelligent and questioning. They were deep and forever… like a night without stars.

He was reading me... An easy task, I think.

I have never been able to hide anything—I feel so guilty about everything. I giggle helplessly if I think I'm getting away with something. Or if I'm accused of something I would do, but didn't—it's like I get hysterical because I'm guilty of being willing to have done it.

Ever play the card game "Bullshit?" I can't.

Anyway, I was right to assume this was his way of offering me the room.

From my folded hands, I looked up his body, madly wanting to put my mouth on his beautiful neck and collarbone. If he had sensed it, felt the same way, and acted upon it… I have no doubt, I would have denied him nothing.

My response was, "When can I come back with my things?"

He smiled. There was something guarded and still somehow sincere about it—this was true for those amazing eyes… and his personality.

It took about a year for me to be myself with him, completely.

By the time I turned 20, we were close.

I remember the first time he kissed me… his hand, from my shoulder, glided smoothly up my neck until it held my jaw. His other hand stealthily found its place on the other side. He kissed me gently, but hungrily. I tasted his mouth inside and out, breaking away long enough to kiss his neck and jaw. When our lips found each other, he held my face more firmly, I assumed, so I wouldn't leave again. When we broke apart, he smiled at me. I laughed a little, breathlessly. I asked him if he wanted to help me fold towels.

Too soon, and unexpectedly, things got complicated—I felt the energy of severe weather in him.

I watched helplessly this beautiful creature enter a downward spiral of self-destruction.

Man vs Self is the cruelest of duels.
It often manifests itself in Man vs Man's Past.
The only way for victory in Man vs Past is to be able to recognize Past as something that didn't have to have any power anymore.

He wasn't the first person who tried to drug the presence of his past self to win, at least, temporarily.

He tried to be close to me—but we were never "alone". And I think he hated himself for not being able to get over "it".

What a miserable hours they were, when he told me what "it" was—or who did it and who he told about it and who did nothing.

I confided in him about my friends—that I couldn't think of anyone I was close to who hadn't been hurt that way—one way or another.

I told him that it didn't matter if we never had sex. Our relationship wouldn't feel any less intimate.

After all, that wasn't what brought us together.

I told him we'd take our time and deal with "never" when it happened.

Feb 5 5:50pm

Rather than pile on the miles to avoid it, it looks like I'll have to face a town tomorrow. I messed up...

It should be alright though... I am all but alone in this world. My "realm", by default.

I wish the empress in me was not so fatalistic... I suppose, she only exists because she is.

Feb 6 4:22pm

I passed through a long since compromised road block and a number of army vehicles. The signs there were unreadable. I keep my eyes peeled for weapons, but if there are they surely lie under winter.

The closer I got to town, the buildings squeezed in together, nearer and nearer—the first sign that I was getting close to somewhere I didn't want to be.

The second sign was for a speed limit of 45.

The third sign was painted on the side of, what had been, a really nice two story home—in huge letters that almost filled the entire side of the structure:

THE END HAS COME

The SUV I got, from the home near the tiny house Grasshopper invaded, has a digital compass. I'm in this trouble now because, apparently, have focused too much on keeping it heading south and not paying enough attention to maps.

The speed limit signs say 45. Obvious warning signs of city limits.

I was seeing a lot of vandalism and sarcastic graffiti and miserable ironic signs. Bible verses posted on mailboxes, vehicles, scrawled across the sides of houses.

Like—

> *"Watch therefore: for ye know not what day your Lord cometh."*

—painted on the side of a minivan in someone's yard.

In the lawn in front of a church, the Bulletin read:

> *"And we know that we are of God, and the whole world lieth in wickedness."*

I slowly depressed the brakes. I came to a stop near the walkway to the church's front doors.

The church itself was vandalized—windows smashed, obscene drawings and gross, rhetorical messages were addressed to people of faith. These things existed in the peripheral alone; I was focused on the human remains heaped on its front steps.

Remains piled *everywhere*.

I couldn't tell if they were stacked intentionally, or if the poor wretches died there. In the snow, in their decay, in their tangled mass... it was impossible to tell. There were a lot of them. Maybe sixty or seventy people in front of the door, alone. The folds of their bodies and crevasses between each other were filled with drifted snow, smoothing the mass—all but a few outstretched hands.

A horrible thought occurred to me, that in the spring this mass would come "alive"... that they were not finished. That they were not finished hunting. I crept along, unable to take my eyes off the wretched business left there.

On the side of the church, someone scrawled a verse, marked Mathew 24:29. It read:

"Immediately after the tribulation of those days shall the sun be darkened and the moon shall not give her light, and the stars shall fall from heaven and the powers of the heavens shall be shaken."

Then after:

"So we're all screwed."

The city lay beyond a dense line of trees and about a block of houses.

I passed the city limits sign. The name had been altered to include the word "dead" and the population had been marked out with a big "Ø."

I was really impressed with how constructively people used their time… idiots always make time to prove it.

A 30mph speed sign was married to the city limits sign. You could have shred zucchini on the points where countless bullets exited through the metal. Like many things before, I couldn't help but stare at it.

On a plastic, sand weighed post in the center of the street, a large sign said "Camp F". Something like an ice fishing house stood directly behind it. Flanking that, were roadblocks. Kitty corner from this intersection was an elementary school. Now mangled tents were arranged within the large fenced yard. A few were standing—though some of the frames were bent and/or the canvases torn.

Indications of military involvement or control were mixed into the derelict section of town…martial law, I'm sure.

I got out and picked up one end of the road block and rotated it so it was parallel with the sidewalk.
I didn't feel rushed back to the truck.

There was emptiness here, though I realized it might be false, I wasn't frightened. This may seem like an inappropriate term to use for an environment like this, but it felt peaceful. With a crashed helicopter there, razor wire strung up over there, a giant gun staring down at me from the top of a Humvee, the fire blackened skeleton of a home… and it felt peaceful.

In the snow and with the disorder, I felt like I'd walked onto the set of a nuclear fallout movie.

Everything was *different* to me, but maybe normal for cities…

The truck's engine idled smoothly—the sound was out of place.
I was out of place. I was an alien.
It had been so long.
Towns existed in the distance... like the sun.

I got back in the SUV and slowly passed through the barricade.

A map was posted on the side of the "fish house," which was actually much longer than it looked. Though it was only about 5 feet wide it was probably 30 feet long. The long side hosted a tattered map. It was a map of the city, but with new internal boundaries and new names and purposes for the buildings. These poor people had probably, and rightfully, assumed the structures here would always be just what they'd always been. Maybe a business would change ownership… maybe the house next door would become a pet groomer's or daycare, but the transformation—doubtlessly under martial law—was absent of warmth and personal considerations. These people had days or only hours to figure out a way to gain control of society and protect it.

I don't envy them…

I was entering Camp F.

Crystal Lake and Arawak were in Camp E ↯

From the map key, it looked like *this* area was for out-of-towners.

There was an area for internationals too…and an assembly area strictly for people without identification,

An orphan's tent,
Senior Citizens and Disabled,
The Jail was called a Detention Center.

When I turned off the truck, *his* song was playing, *Gone Away*, by Cold. I climbed out of the vehicle to see it this "Survivor Support Station" better.

The "No Clearance Area", a small sign said, was where one should go to report suspicious behavior, fever, bites, crimes, and disorderly people, among other things.

If this place had survived, I'm sure that would be quickly corrupted.

Camp meetings were strictly prohibited unless organized by camp administrators. Apparently any organized group wasn't allowed. The list of rules was almost as tall as the "gatehouse"— I guess more so than a fish house.

"Out-of-towners"… the unfortunate position of the majority who end up at these stations—I don't even have to know it, to know it. It gives reason to the look of this section of the camp. The efficiency driven disregard for *things*… the discarding of identity and history… What does that look like? Like a tornado hit an all-state flea market.

These things those poor people couldn't bear to leave behind—

I heard Mr. Ages scratching at the window so I let him out. He doesn't wear a leash anymore.

We went deeper into the camp. Down each side street were identical tents. Large signs, like name tags, showed what buildings functioned as, in their last days serving people.

I accidently kicked a book, half buried in the snow—it turned out not to be a book at all when loose photographs scattered freely, like dry leaves—getting caught on the remains of other people's lives or blowing to an unknown end on the suddenly rising wind.

I saw smiles, carousing friends and family photos spiral and fly away like they were sucked into a frost giant's inward breath. There was s school picture,
A new baby,
A Christmas morning…
Then there wasn't.

The wind sighed in my ears. The same gust whistled as it poured through the broken windows of a small diner. I heard the fluttering of the photographs, but could not see where they went… their white backs, scrawled with names and dates, were lost entirely against Winter.

I was using a long sleeved t-shirt for a scarf and I raised one wrist to my eyes.

I needed to see more.

People were supposed to go to these places.
There was nothing on the radio when I tried it, but I knew that sometime, somewhere, the airwaves were live, telling people to come here for help. People like Mickey and Janice.

Where were the people?

I think the bodies outside town were survivors that didn't make it inside the Camp. There were a lot of ways for the people who came here to be fucked over.

The lists on the gatehouse might explain why so many went to the church:

-If you came you *had to* register, you couldn't leave.
-You couldn't get rations without a registration card.
-You couldn't get rations without a "housing" assignment.
--You can't get a housing assignment without being allowed inside.
-You wouldn't be allowed inside until there was room.

The punishments were grotesque and probably lethal— eventually—for most of the "crimes" listed. If money meant anything, I'd put a lot on the bet that there were good Samaritans at the church back there trying to supplement what people weren't getting from the camp. Maybe they couldn't keep up with the demands or perhaps the violence of people doing anything to live.

But that didn't explain where all the bodies were of the people inside the ~~compound~~ camp.

So I looked harder.
I felt stupid, horrible and horrified when I realized where they'd gone—they were under the snow.

The street signs showed evidence of violence—bent to hell and/or riddled with bullet holes. There was very old blood on everything. Windows smashed out. Burned houses. One section of the chain link fence was collapsed outward.

The front doors of the school were broken—one hanging like a small child on its parent's hand. The other lay mostly covered in a drift that freely entered the school hall. The lockers—they looked so short—didn't have any locks on them. It was summer, when this all began… the best time in a child's life. I took a left at the next intersection.

I was suddenly very conscious of two things—neither my rifle or shotgun were with me and I didn't lock the vehicle's doors. Somehow, I brushed those thoughts aside. In retrospect, it's frightening how easily I did that.

But the need to see was stronger….   I *needed* to see.

I'd done things I shouldn't have done, as far as safety goes, but I didn't feel like it was as risky as it probably should have.

Am I adapting or is my give-a-damn going the way of the dodo?

Never abandon caution.

Only so many possessions were allowed—what they could fit in their tent.

There were areas that appeared to exist for dumping and sorting excess items. The land of "out-of-towners". It was starting to remind me of a concentration camp.

Turning onto the next street brought me face to face with a graveyard—a graveyard of cars. Campers, trailers, trucks. A supermarket—now an "Items Consolidation and Trade Station", lost its parking lot to the vehicles of the people; if only from this camp…maybe others'.

The lot was packed so tightly you would have to take a vehicle from an end to get access to the next. A child would struggle to get through a window, if they could at all. I'd bet there is gas plenty of those vehicles... reaching it would be a bitch.

I put the thought in my back pocket and moved on.

Shortly after I found a busy body sitting on the lip of a city planter. His eyes sometimes moved. I don't ~~always~~ know what's going on in their heads, but even for a zombie he looked despondent, just like the one I'd come across before...
His presence didn't excite Mr. Ages. We were feet from him before it was clear he wasn't just another body. Likely none of them were.

He was little more than a solid ghost. He was eaten on the neck, shoulder and had completely lost an ear, but everything that was left was young and handsome and gone—as gone as gone can be—

You'll never catch me

—he was helpless.

He managed to look up at me and almost straightened a little. Almost.

I reached out—Mr. Ages made a sound, almost a whimper, uneasy sound—I brushed snow off the man's hand and found a warm yellow-gold band devoutly gripping the gray blue, blackening flesh.

"You came here with your family?" I asked him.
I almost left my hand on his hand, but I stepped back—why take the chance?

The dead, busy bodies, sometimes exhibit pattern behavior. Sometimes they learn. An elbow happens to bump a doorknob—suddenly two dozen think that this one must have tried to get in, because there *must* have been something living in there. Suddenly that two dozen is shoving past the one, to get at whatever was in that house.

This dead man didn't know what to do with himself. He was cold and had no memories—or whatever stirred those habitual rituals.

He was lost.

"If your family is alive, while they won't know, they are hoping you aren't suffering. If they are gone, really gone, you should be with them."

I crouched enough to meet his eyes.
He was trying to open his mouth.
I felt tears rising.

I asked him and wanted to know so badly:

"Is your soul in there?"

I reached out again and put my palm under his jaw and held it with my fingertips to his throat. I really felt, behind the weirdness in his eyes, that something was there. And when I drove the screwdriver up into his brain, through the soft spot my two longest fingers found, I watched the energy leave. Whether the energy of who he was or the energy that brought him back.

I should have killed that other one.

My fingers supported the jaw until it dropped as low as it was ever going to.

Then, I was going to leave.

Standing up and turning away, I was faced with a street that made my eyes widen. I felt a jarring beat in my heart—responding in surprise, wonder and fear.

This side of town, the street, sloped downward. What got my attention was little compared to what I had to digest when I reached the top of the hill and could see down into it.

It was hard to tell if it was a flood or a tornado that was responsible for the devastation I was seeing below me—through the snow and filth—I just couldn't tell. Tall buildings slumped like they'd collapsed on their knees and put their heads to the ground.

What buildings remained standing were dirty up to their waists. A flood could do that—a bad storm could do that.

I was apprehensive about descending into this part of the city—like entering another level of Hell. No inferno—just cold and bleak and wasted. A sneak preview of the world without man—and of what our ruins will look like. They will find the bodies mummified, huddled on the floor in closets. They will see the blown out heads. They will see evidence of many families' last stands. They will find a mass of bodies in front of a church. Somewhere in the distance, in the northern Midwest, they will find houses with piles of bodies heaped around back—all of them killed by the same hammer or screwdriver.

I wonder who will see them.

Who will explore them?

Will they have any idea how we lived?

If I knew the answer, would it reveal how much of history is merely guessing?

I walked carefully down the icy slope of cracking pavement. Ahead of me lay an improvised and crudely compromised fence to Camp D. The buildings level off with me as I descend. I slowly submit to their shadows as I enter the ruined part of the city.

Past a barely distinguishable out-of-state school bus, I see little bodies frozen in the shallow rerouted river that cuts through the city. The brown ice is rough with tall frost forests. Little fingers and small hands rise out of the dirty ice like fins and frothy spray of water creatures in a miniature world. I can make no sense of what happened here.

The children are mixed among frozen things and larger frozen people. But it is mostly children.

The bus is battered. It'd left paint along the buildings east of it. "Cross something you shouldn't have?" I said aloud. I don't think I sound like me.

I scanned the ice.

I guessed it was probably only a couple feet deep and frozen solid. A short hike proved I was right when I predicted there would be more bodies down the street, downstream, sorted out of the water by a couple more military hummers and a sturdy road block. They looked like a beaver dam of frozen, depleted flesh, and wasted life.

Above me, mannequins boasted their infallibility through one of only a few intact windows.

Perfect lips formed perfect smiles at the wasteland in front of them. They stood with their hands on their hips or extended them casually over crumpled bodies. They would remain still and fearless even if the dead overcame… and overlooked them. I'm here, I thought to the plastic gods.

The world isn't yours yet.

I was in a business district. Bakeries and bookshops. A coffee shop on a corner—there, a busy body slumped, stiff with cold in the doorway. A screen printing shop. Tattoos. A craft store. Antiques. Chocolate shop. Souvenirs. A lot of notices from the Powers That Be.

I felt the pull of my old life drawing me to books—not that the pull of coffee and antiques wasn't there, but availability and practicality sorta numbed the interest. But books…books could give me new life.

They were always good, at least, for escaping mine.

After the devastation, I wondered how much there was to salvage anyway. Very few windows left. Weather had spoiled and soiled almost everything it touched. The integrity of the building's structure was iffy. Not worth the risk.

Beyond this row of buildings, a wall of blowing snow concealed the city beyond. Through the now strong gusts of wind, I dissolved into the curtain of white. As the breath of winter died and drew itself in for the next blow, I saw buildings eaten and broken… like us. I saw a land ravaged by cruel weather.

What's left?

Not just here. Anywhere.

Can I really hope there is somewhere to go?

Looking at this raised new and old concerns—new problems.
What happens to towns when there's no one to care for them?

What happens when there's no one to fight the fires?
Who sends out the tornado warnings?
Who's going to get you breathing?
Who's going to start your heart?
Deliver your babies?

Make babies.

Take care of us when we're old?
What happens to our warheads?
What about all the people who should have been?
The people who were already in hospitals?
The pets in the pet shop? Animals in the zoo?

No cops. No laws.

No one to keep an eye on things. No one to keep track.
No one to teach us.
No one to clean up.
No one to bury all these dead.
No way to put to rest all the ghosts.

This town is a ghost—as dead as the graffiti renamed it.

There was nothing more for me to see. I wanted to leave, but it
was hard to, too. Avoiding towns kept me from seeing.

Now I was <u>seeing</u>.

I'd seen enough.

I turned on my heel to leave. One wall stood stubbornly among the rubble. Brushed with white paint on the red brick, it said:

"But he that endures to the end, the same shall be saved."

I stared dumbly at it as the wind rose up and the swirling whiteness ate the words and the sounds of cries this stupid girl couldn't keep down. The brutal, howling gusts tore away every simper, muting the world… and me. This stupid girl, crying and screaming and feeling that somehow the words were making demands of me.

I ran until I fell and then I walked the rest of the way back to my vehicle.

I turned the MP3 player on again, when we got back in the truck. Shaking violently, I fumbled with the shifting gears. My internal being answering the wall with one awful and most common question:

Who am I to be the last?

I did a U-turn in reverse—I couldn't bring myself to drive on the remains of the living and their lives.

Fear, by Sarah McLachlan was ending. *Pretty Donna*, by Collective Soul played next, on shuffle. I always wished that song was longer. I invested my concentration into driving and listening to the songs that played. I needed an out. I needed to get away from myself.

I was fighting tears—making gross sounds in my throat. My vision warped as my eyes filled. I blinked hard and squeezed them out to clear them. My contacts burned—I should put on my glasses. How much solution do I have left?

My consciousness was so congested with thoughts and feelings that, at first, I didn't realize what one thing made me feel so helpless and moved to submit to them.

With all of that I couldn't yet digest—my ears were eating *Nothing Left to Say* the Imagine Dragons song—I felt something in me breaking.

It's dark. My headlights grab at unseen dangers and 40mph seems like the speed of light. In a way, it is.

I see eyes flash in the night—most of them are likely deer and small critters. The rest? I don't know about them.
I end the day to *A.D.I.D.A.S.*

It's 20 degrees F.

Feb 7 1:48pm

I never slept the whole night by *him,* my boyfriend—the one I lived with…

He wanted me to want him.
But it horrified him to be wanted.

Sometimes we fell asleep on the couch or in bed watching movies on his laptop, but once sleep set in, it didn't last long enough to count.

He was restless—it wasn't just the drugs—he was unsettled.

If he tossed and turned, eventually I had to leave so I could sleep. It bothered him. If I told him why I had to leave, it bothered him. If he got up and paced and paced and paced and I asked him what was wrong—everything was wrong.

I couldn't hold him when he was like that, any more than that poor creature in town.
And I learned, again, to shrink.

And I learned to yearn.
All the good wants were there and I was in a home with someone that wanted me there, but it started to get cold—even when I felt things were good.

It wasn't because we weren't sleeping together—neither of us was in a state of mind for that. I was learning about being close to people because of him. For him to believe that being close could be safe and good was a greater challenge than mine.

Love wanted to be there.

We cared for each other more than I'd ever cared for anyone. And I yearned. I missed him—I felt him slipping away every time an embrace ended. I felt like he was beads of oil on a pan of water and I was trying to hold him all together. So I held him all the time.
When he cried, I felt pieces of him trying to fly away through the gaps where we did not touch.

When he was high, it was like holding in an explosion.

I couldn't hold it.

When he too could not hold it, he broke things, sometimes tearing the place apart—and scared the hell out of me.

One time I called Carrie to see if I could spend the week with her. I locked him out of my room and cried until I fell asleep. Somewhere in there were his words, beseeching through the thin door, but I could barely understand them.

He listened quietly the next morning while I told him I was going to go home for a week—he raised his eyebrows a little at this and searched my eyes—I explained that this meant seeing my friends, not my family. Obviously.

He looked down.

I told him that I would see him Sunday night. I held his face and made him look at me.

"I'm coming back," I promised. "This isn't the end of anything, but I don't know what to do when it's like that."

I didn't want to say, when "you're" like that.

"I'll stop." He meant the drugs.

He couldn't live in his mind without them—not all the time.

"I'm not worried," I lied.

I put my forehead to his. I didn't know I was crying until then—when I bent forward I felt hot wetness track down my face. I felt his tears run into the "L's" my hands made along his beautiful jaw. "We don't have to compromise."

The only thing I'd change about him were the old wounds that I could only wait to heal.

And I could.

I felt "I love you" fill every fiber of my being and light up every part of my soul—before him, my friends were the only ones lighting candles in there—I <u>love</u> them, but it was different, something so big that I couldn't speak.

I looked into his eyes. My mouth clamped on sobs coming up my throat—even as more tears came I forced a smile, albeit a weak one, as evidence we'd be okay.

I left into a hot and humid August morning and returned on a hotter Sunday afternoon.

When I opened the door, I knew he'd *quit*.
He'd quit everything.

My things, my purse and luggage, seemed to fall off me. I bashed my hip against the kitchen table as I went through the room. I looked at the chair where I left him, as if he should have still been there.

"Where'd you go?"

My knees were watery.

I felt tears that must have only lain dormant since our "fight" come alive—just like the dead would do in a few years.

I smelled it before I could see it—It's a smell you never forget.

I couldn't see him, only the blood. Everlasting blood.

I'm sure I looked right at him and I couldn't see him. It was like being blind, only instead of seeing blackness I saw blood. A starburst of blood on the wall. I am now only vaguely aware that I had been screaming since the very moment the smell struck me.

Sometime in there I called the police, let them in and told them about the "fight." All the while I felt like I hadn't said anything—that I hadn't moved from the spot, like a plant in a time lapse or something. I was in a time lapse.

Is there anyone we can call, someone asked.

I could barely shake my head. I wanted to say, "They killed him! Everything is because of what they did—

But I was the one who was with him. What should I have said differently? What should I not have said? What should I have? I feel like I was the straw that destroyed that beautiful, forsaken, broken creature—

And I felt like *Jesus died for me*
Why? Why? WHY! Fuck. So fucking worthless. So fucking nothing!
I dunno.

I felt everything. *Everything*. When someone dies, they aren't the only ones that see their lives pass before their eyes... In that, I think the sum of their importance in our life. I think, this tells us how much it's going to hurt.

At some point I was screaming—or wailing—or howling—it was a sound, a terrible sound that scared me. I felt like it was ripping out of my throat. I screamed "God" for what felt like minutes. I cried his name so many times that, eventually, I could only creak it out. I felt angry.

I felt

everything.

My head felt like it was hemorrhaging, swelling, exploding—
my lips felt puffy and I couldn't breathe out of my nose.

I was dully aware of the constant presence of a paramedic who
didn't leave me until my nearest friends arrived. I changed
hands. I heard Patrick say, "I've got her." I felt the paramedic's
hand relax and leave my shoulder. I smelled Marie holding me.
I felt the car ride. I lay in a bed. I lost time.

In a couple days, I guess, it seemed like one night, I wanted to
go back.

His family was picking through everything, even my things.
They were moving stuff out. They were gonna take my car.
They didn't know about me, because he had nothing to do with
them.

Marie immediately got involved—I watched them throw away
things he loved. Patrick called the police. I heard someone say
his uncle's name—I found the monster with my eyes and hated.
I wanted to kill him. I could have killed him.

I recovered some of my things—my car.
I was not entitled to him. I was not family—I wasn't known to
the family and I wasn't on the lease. I had no right to him.
They took his things.

They took his body.

While I know it's what he wanted, they cremated him, but in
doing so they took away so much as knowing where he
rested—or with who. I didn't even know when or where the
funeral was. If the funeral was.

But I knew what they did to him before he left us.

I felt like the whole world should have stopped when he did—
and it made me hurt and mad and so confused when it didn't.
Didn't they know what was gone?
Or how?
~~Or why?~~
He quit.
You quit things you hate—if you can quit them.

He quit.

I thought we could do anything, eventually.

What else did we have, but time?

Feb 8 7:22am

I am staring down a massive bridge.

It crosses the Mississippi into Missouri.

I hate bridges. I don't like heights or water. Yippee.

What happens if I'm out there and they amass around me? The
coast looks clear, for now. The coast, as a matter of fact, looks
really clear. Far back along the river banks are signs of
flooding that's sometime receded. Perhaps the mother of the
destruction I saw before.

Well, rather than putting it off any longer—gonna just get it
over with.

You ever hear about that bull shark that was found in the
Mississippi? I wonder how far upstream it got.

9:49am

Most the right hand turns are telling me I'm really close to where that doctor was studying this. The one from the newspaper who had seen it in apes or chimps or whatever. All of that was just a couple hours away, in St. Louis. That guy plunged headfirst into trying to tackle this problem, according to the article.

Is it because he *knew* how bad it was going to be?

I wonder how much he knew. Or knows, I suppose. He could be alive… Shall we check the survival statistics?

Within a week, he already knew enough to tell us that it wasn't just humans passing around doses of reality cancer. Maybe he was responsible?

I don't believe that. This shit didn't come out of a test tube. Anyway, it's just weird to be so close.

Maybe, someday, there will be answers to all of this, here.

Feb 9 4:04pm

I stopped earlier because I thought I saw something down by the opposite side of the river. I thought it was a deer, but I couldn't have really been looking.

I am unreasonably far from my truck now, but I feel safe.

Mr. Ages is laying in the snow and weeds beside me. This is so stupid to be in this position—foolish. I don't care.

I have been laying here for three hours and Mr. Ages hasn't made a peep. He's watching too.

At first I thought it was a busy body, but he's not. I couldn't tell by looking at him until I used my binoculars. Eventually I would have known, when he started doing things they don't do.

I named him Neville.

I think the shambled, nondescript mess of branches and trash is his shelter. I can't tell what shape he's in because he's wearing a million layers and his hair is unkempt. It almost looks like he does try to keep his beard at bay. So there's a knife or a scissor down there somewhere…

Even before I saw the "camp", I saw him wade out into the partially frozen river and close his fist in the air. With fist still raised, he moved back to the shore. Then fist over fist, in what looked like thin air, he pulled in a fish. I saw a limb bouncing on the trees behind him, where a fishing line was tied.

I said "A-ha" out loud, but not loud. I was startled by the sound of me addressing me. I talk to Mr. Ages, but I realized then that somewhere along the line here I stopped talking to myself.

I don't know what that means after having worried so long about doing it too much.

This world demands quiet.

His world demands that too. He doesn't make a sound.

He laid the fish on a log—he must have broken its back or something because it wasn't flopping around at all. He waded back in, without splashing, and let the current eat the lure. I noticed two other things then too. There was a branch sticking out of the water, that kept the line off the bank, and I also spotted the bobber.

He went back to his fish. He didn't start a fire.

5:11pm

I can tell nothing about him.

His age… his hair is mostly dark, but it's hard to tell, it's filthy. I almost wonder if it isn't really blonde or light brown like mine.

It's hard to even know what ethnicity he is.

The binoculars aren't good enough to show me everything. They show me another human who is alone. And this time I know about the person first.

This is intriguing.

He is intriguing. I have seen four others before him—I knew no more about them than I do him. Even with the three that I—I wondered what they'd been through. How they came together.

I watch him go about his business—it has the sureness of routine.

I think, regardless of how filthy he looks, he is taking care of himself and he is capable. Whether he always was, or this situation made him so, was as impossible to tell as whether or not he had fillings in his teeth.

I feel bad for him.

I watch him long enough to know, he is more alone than me.

6:37pm

I've decided to move on after Neville very quickly and unexcitedly dispatched a number of busy bodies. Afterward, he propped the small bloody pickaxes, like climbing or excavating picks?, against the log where he was sitting and resumed eating fish number two—even with the corpses stink a mere ten feet behind him.

He is clearly a dangerous man—what he does with it determines whether he is good or bad... can even a good man be trusted?

Your eyes only give you clues. Only clues.

There's a verse in the bible that I can't stop thinking about: "Take heed that no man deceive you."

Still I wonder, I *must* wonder what it would be like to find the sweetest kiss in the middle of Hell.

Feb 10 7:56am

I can't believe it's come to that again... I would do anything right now to not be alone.

Now it's just me and regret again. But in a weird way you are with me right now, aren't you?

I wonder where I am. Do I? Probably not.

Some people would say it's an antifeminist idea to "need" a man. But right now I feel *that*, that is exactly what I need—like what's the point without a man?

When the loneliness and shame subsides, I can reevaluate what I need in life…again.

There's a lot of regret right now.

I should have been going through this with *him*.

I fucked up. I lost. Maybe he was my only chance. I don't think fate is concrete, just intended. But I think the odds are, now, that I won't get another chance. Not even if someone else was destined for me.

Fate is like Human Resources. It makes you think you can go to it with your problems, but that's only to keep you from fucking with its plan to keep business like usual.

Neither is on your side.

Neither, I believe, is infallible.

Well… definitely not now.

There's no fucking HR or PR or PC or PBS or BBQ or B&W. There's lots of BS and BO and *BB's.

(*Busy Bodies)

Feb 11 2:49pm

The freeway exit slopes deep and curls down, and to the right, where a Wal-Mart parking lot grabs it. I would love to see what I could find there. I was thinking about it when the dogs came. Probably forty of them. They are chasing down something small, too bloody and too far away to distinguish.

They are biting each other and fights break out among them. They are thin and miserable and ugly.

They've noticed us. They are running, but not away.

Shit.

3:24pm

I wish I could describe what Mr. Age's face looked like watching them.

I might be projecting, I don't think so, but it was easy to imagine that he was probably feeling what I did when I watched other people not acting "like people".

There was something about the feral animals that makes calling them dogs seem really inappropriate.

They belong to the wild now.

Feb 12 3:41pm

I'm not gonna lie, it really looks delicious. It smells smoky and meaty. There are actually strips of meat packed into luscious looking gravy.

I tried to be enthusiastic about the first bite, because it looked sooo good, but the smell lied about the flavor, which was pretty bland, but not disgusting. It's slimy.

So I wonder if appetite and cravings are largely based on smell for dogs.

Dog food keeps a long time, unopened. This particular kind still has a couple years on it.

I think I could like it.

I will *not* be eating any with carrots or peas. And for the first time in my life I'll get to have "lamb". At least I won't have any preconceived ideas of how it should be.

Feb 16 11:19am

I'm at a country greenhouse shop. In the soft, filtered light I sit on a twin-sized bed of dirt. The air is warm. The dirt is soft, like powder. I feel the heat it's collected through the fabric of my jeans. My bum is warm and comfortable. Mr. Ages lays on his side on the earth next to me. He has fallen asleep. Front feet extended and crossed at the wrists, one paw jumps and seems to wave like a hand, while he dreams. I want to reach out and touch him, but it's selfish to bother him. I think about Neville. I wonder where he is and what he is doing. I wonder where he has been. I wonder, even if he were not the best person, if it would be worth it, so not to be alone. . . Does he monopolize my thoughts, simply because he exists?

I found seeds and a lot of other useful gardening equipment. I'm going to take the seeds with me.

I like it here. I feel something good here, even as I have descended deeper into the world of freezing cold and ice. I don't care. I hope I won't be traveling much longer, so what does it matter?

Something almost feels like it's saying, "What took you so long?"

    … maybe even,

                      "Welcome Home."

Not to be cynical, but that would be the first time in my life when anything that said, "Welcome Home" wasn't synonymous with a bad thing… at least, somewhere I definitely didn't want to be.

I think I've found what I'm looking for, but there's only one way to know—to find exactly what I'm looking for. The nearest town is Poplar Bluff. I have an idea about how to find the perfect home. What I would do in my other life, a normal life (if I didn't have internet)—I'm going to check the paper.

5:02pm

I'm sitting in a room in the Relax Motel in Poplar Bluff. Other than dust, it is untouched. The beds are made and, under the comforter, they even smell pretty fresh. There's no vandalism whatsoever. The little bars of soap and extra toilet paper are still wrapped. The soap smells lovely when I tear open a corner of the slightly glossy, cream colored paper—I'm already making plans to find the housekeeping supply closet. I imagine fresh comforters in dry cleaning bags. Toilet paper in crinkly tissue wrapping and all the shampoo and other soaps I could ever need or want. The linen and toiletries will be fully stocked when I move in.

I parked the SUV a couple of rooms down, so if someone comes looking, they look in the wrong place first. If they, for some reason, saw which room I went to, or returned to, and went to the right room first, it would be the wrong thing if they want to live.

I feel stronger than ever before, even though my whole body is full of aches or injuries, and I periodically lose feeling in my left arm and it hurts to move it because of the stab wound behind my shoulder, and my forearms are riddled with so many cuts from the window I crawled out of that I look like I was mauled by a tiger—despite or because of these things I feel more determined than ever to make it.

Light is streaming in through the unboarded glass and I am falling in love with this place.

After collecting and scouring through newspapers and real state ads, I think I found a house about nine miles out of town. If it's all that the ad boasts it—I might be home.

Sweet merciful heaven. . . my journey might be over.

I reach into my pack and close my hand on my careworn copy of *The Road*. I thank it. I thank Mr. McCormac.

An idle mind is the engine of living zombies and the mechanism of mental and emotional collapse. Would I have even been strong enough to make this journey without that book? Would I have even been strong enough to face my old life? It's hard to be ungrateful for even the little things, after exploring only a few moments in the world of that man and boy. I think it may be impossible.

I squeeze the curled pages in my hand, like it's a hand. It is.

I love on Mr. Ages and play with him a little, which I almost never do. We have time for it now.

In my gut, I feel that we will soon have time to live.

I beckoned my companion and we went out into the dazzling sunlight and brisk winter air. I raised one hand to shade my eyes, when I squint I smile involuntarily. . . then voluntarily.

I pull on one of Mr. Ages' satiny ears. When he looks up, the sun is also in his eyes—they are sparkling and his mouth is hanging open. Involuntarily, the squinting and panting spreads a smile across his face too. No. *Voluntarily*.

8:41pm

I just got back from a little place just off Highway 60. It was for sale and all the furniture, but the beds, were gone; so I could really see what I was getting into, by peering into its also unboarded windows—besides the emptiness, I also saw a hall almost completely lined with bookshelves.

When I get settled, I'm going to try to adopt copies of the books I left behind. It *will* feel like home when the shelves are stuffed with books.

Tonight I'm going to make a checklist of every title I left behind and need to reacquire. I'm going to make two shopping lists: One, of everything I need. The other, of everything I want.

Needing and wanting is the difference between surviving and living.

The property is sprawling. There is a small shed and a large detached garage. The house is single level with a fireplace and a pond. The house isn't really visible from the road. There is plenty of yard to turn into a garden. It was overwhelmingly obvious—I can do a lot with this place.

I have a few ideas for fortifying it without it looking obviously occupied or fortified.

I'm going to get a metal door and a new lock set because I'm sure I will have to break in and I want to have my own keys.

I am planning to break through the window on the front door to let myself in, since I have doubts about the integrity of the door that's there right now. I also want to have reinforced doors on the inside. I'm not sure how I'm going to get all the things done that I have in mind, but I'll figure it out.

I have to.
I'm really excited.
I am *happy*. I am happy. And I feel so... so close to *living*.

There is something vibrant in my chest, right in the spot that gets tight when you panic. My spirit?

I am so relieved.

Mr. Ages is smiling and content. He ran around like a fawn on speed, checking everything out too. Aggressively marking everything. He knows, as well as I do, that that is our place now.

I just asked him what he thinks. He's strung out on the other bed. He only bothered to roll his head at me and wag his tail a little. He's exhausted in the most wonderful way. Blissfully.

I'm going to go jump on him. I'm thinking a belly flop.

I'm too excited to sleep, so I'm not going to let him either.

I end up sprawled out on the bed beside him. We're both filthy and grimy on the practically clean comforter and that makes me happy too. I am too tired after jumping once that I just lay where I am. After he pulled his back legs out from under me, he just lay where he was too.

I know it won't take long before the elements take their toll on all the homes, without people to care for them. It won't take long before plant life starts to grow over dirt roads, driveways and force itself through the cracks in pavement and cement, without anyone there to fight it back.

It won't be long before I remember more days without people than with them. Then the memory of "people" will be like ghost stories we survivor's tell ourselves. In a few decades the human race will be wiped out, unless there are any children surviving or born.

I know these things.

Undoubtedly, they will each come to pass—if everything continued to go wrong, but it hasn't. Not for me.

Who am I to be the last? I *know* I'm not. I can't ever be.

This is not the end.

I'm alive.

I'm alive.

I'm living.

I've got my earbuds in. I crank up the volume to the acoustic version of Matisyahu's *Live Like a Warrior*.

I'm not afraid.
Hardly can I believe it… but I am *not*.
Mr. Ages will let me know if anything is wrong.
I trust him. I can depend on him.

Being able to do that is harder than to love someone. I've loved him for what feels like all time. It doesn't feel, anymore, that he was ever *not* in my life. Which reinforces the theory that he was sent by God.

I think I have actually met my guardian angel.

And I *do* trust him.

After all these nights of bio-warfare I should question if that is wise.

Goodnight. ☺

Feb 17 7:19pm

I found a travel bathroom kit. I melted some snow and have just brushed the hell out of my teeth. I feel instantly healthier. I am a little troubled that my gums bled by one molar.

What else is breaking down, I wonder.

Marie used to say, if she wanted an instant goddess makeover she'd shave her legs and lose five pounds at the same time.

That woman didn't worry about "letting herself go."

She was never stupid enough to give all of herself away. She knew herself so well. I always admired that about her. If she didn't feel like shaving her legs for five months, why the hell should she? Why the hell should anyone?

Can we have it better now? Can we learn from our mistakes?

All of those stupid somethings don't matter anymore. Our lives have been whittled down to what matters most… In this world, what is the value of money? What is the value of extensions and hair plugs? What is the value of popularity? Of FB "Likes"? Of jewels and jewelry? Of wearing designer clothes?

In this world, what is the value of compassion? Of skill and wisdom? Of hard work? Of industriousness? Of bravery? Of cowardice?

Of shaved legs?

I know that it was hard for me to give a damn when I wasn't involved with someone. Who was I doing it for?

Only my capris.

Were I the last living person in the world, would I have any reason to be? Is living for yourself enough, if you are not a sociopath? Do humans have a point or purpose without other people?

I don't know…

I think this dog is my reason to be…   ☺

Feb 18   4:43 pm

He shot him in the head
   He fucking shot him in the head!
The dead were on him by the time I got back — the gun shot brought them
   they ruined him

They ate on him

Did those fuckers think I'd just let it go?
Do they think I'd just leave????

Fucking cowards   COWARDS!
   He fucking shot him
God.

   Oh fuck. Fuck. Fuck!
   Fuck Fuck Fuck
   Fuck FuckFuck

   Fuck it
      Oh God
Oh my God.

   Mr. Ages

They better know to run and hide—but I don't think they do.

People like that are never afraid or they would never do what they do. Even if they try to get away—and maybe they will—I know what *I'd* do, but it's because it's what I do—what I *did*. I'm gonna find them.

If all we're doing is waiting for the inevitable, then I guess what we should really be doing is choosing the best time and way to die.

If I can make them sorry, before they kill me, that is good. Then I can do what I have to do for him, because I can't take the time now, but I hope I get to.

I need to get to, because I need to bury him.

I'm alive right now—I can't bring him back—so why take chances?

Because that dog took chances all the time for me - ALL THE TIME - I can't take the chance of any of them being around, anyway.

I'm going to kill every last one of them—twice.

It's getting dark—I see the smoke of their camp. They are in the ravine just about a hundred yards from where they jumped me. They may move on if I wait until morning.

they may try to run away

I can't give him back to God like this. I can't do *anything* right! It's so fucking backwards! I couldn't do anything for him and now Mr. Ages… he wouldn't want to be burned, but I can't – I can't – I can't! I CAN'T!

I CAN'T

I can't give him back to God like this.

They RUINED him!!
Oh God!

He would have wanted to be *buried*—with his face in the dirt—with the earth in his fur. Soiled. And that—so very fucking wonderful to a dog.

But I can't return something I borrowed in this condition. I ~~won't take the chance~~ I can't take the chance that anything should dig him up.

I need to burn him, so nothing can defile him.

this time, *he's* mine. this time I get to do the right thing. this time is not last time, the last time is this time, it's not the right time—fuck time

fuck everything

I *can't* do right by Mr. Ages in the dark—they would see the fire and might surprise me again.

they're in for a surprise

I can't stop laughing. I can't stop shaking. I'm hysterical.

Stop. STOP.

When will it stop???

What do I do? What did I do?? HOW DID I LET THIS HAPPEN???

What can I do!

Who am I?

I'm nothing. I'm nobody. No—I'm a coward. I'm worthless.

He won't be there to protect me—he will be with me—I know he'll be with me. He's with me

Oh God his poor body

They <u>aren't</u> going to leave. They aren't. They aren't. They *aren't*.

I'm gonna make them scream and they're going to die like cowards—I need to believe God will understand.

He knew Mr. Ages better than me—so I'm counting on Him cheering me on. *For I am fearfully and wonderfully made.* Right?

If I face St. Peter in the next few hours and he asks about what I'd done to them. I'll answer, "Hell yes and I'd do it again. I wish I had lived to do worse—unless you can stop me, I'd like to finish the job."

I know he's in heaven and if I want to be with him I really

shouldn't do what I'm going to do, but <u>not</u> doing it doesn't give me any guarantees. Not doing it leaves those monsters to breathe, to prey on someone else, which I think is a sin in itself.

I may already be damned. I could be damned for things I've done. I could be damned for things I haven't done—*I'm so fucking sorry for being so mad! I'm so sorry for hurting you! It's not your fault. It's not your fault. I would have come back. I DID COME BACK!!*

i loved you

Why did you quit? Why? WHY?

I won't. I WON'T!
i can't. I would rather go to hell.

To Saint Peter, I may remind him, "*God already knows.*"

As it says in Psalms somewhere:

I was made secretly in the lowest parts of the earth. God knew me, before I had formed. And in His book they all were written, the days planned for me, when as yet there were none of them.

Today, I'll take my chances.

I was foraging in a gas station parking lot, checking the vehicles. Mr. Ages was some distance off to one side sniffing the underside of a camper.

Out of nowhere—ice and snow crunching and smashing.

A large, dirty, thick hand seized my left wrist and I was slammed to the ground. Something went wrong in my shoulder. His long, filth clogged nails bit into my wrist. But my right hand was full of high carbon steel and when I swung my hammer it blew out the shape of the man's knee and in seconds blackish red started wicking through the fabric.

He flung back like a pigeon with a broken wing, rocking and flapping near the front bumper of a little green Honda Civic. A second man, younger, caught my lower right arm and twisted it until I let go of the hammer. My bag was ripped off my back.

The first, the older, was back, bleeding, crying and furious.

He grabbed my screwdriver and tossed it. They were threatening me. I could barely understand their words. They alluded to others who would also hurt me. Even now, I hear those words as clear as a poet laureate reciting them in a perfectly silent room.

They are words I was meant to remember. I needed to remember there were others, because I was going to survive this, no matter what.

The one I hurt returned the favor—his big boot jumped into my ribs, awaking the slumbering giant of a childhood injury. I gasped out a cry, at the same time, punched in the mouth. My teeth shredded the block of hand.

The man made an awful sound.

I almost giggled.
I'd seen enough ~~end of the world~~ movies to know their
intentions, even *if* intuition hadn't been screaming the same
thing.

The older yanked my belt out and cast it aside while the
slightly younger bastard held my wrists and a fistful of hair. I
could smell traces of feces in their filthy jeans. Their hands
reeked. They smelled sour and rank and faintly burnt, probably
from campfires.

The older standing over me wobbled drunkenly on his ruined
knee. It was nothing that would ever heal.

I was vaguely aware of his penis when it flopped against my
knee. I don't know when he took it out.

In that moment I heard the winding down of his time on earth.

I knew they'd beat me more if I fought—they were probably
going to beat me and kill me anyway, ~~but~~ How could I call my
life worth living if I wasn't going to pay any price to protect it
and the body charged to carry it.

In these matters, the only thing to do is fight.

Suddenly Mr. Ages was hanging on the older man's trunk-like
throat—there was screaming and blood. The younger let go of
me. I kicked the older off. I grabbed my belt by one end and
swung the buckle as hard as I could at the younger's head and
again from the opposite side. He toppled backward on his heels
and I stomped between his open legs as hard as I could.

While the older man struggled with Mr. Ages, I recovered my hammer and screwdriver. I put on my bag. The older man stood, I swung up from knee level with the claw of the hammer and caught him under his exposed testicles. I followed through—a swing hardly interrupted by tearing flesh.

He didn't have time to feel it.

His skull made a melon-like sound when the screwdriver punched it.
The younger disappeared. We needed to too.

I ran for the truck.
I called for Mr. Ages.
I heard him run with me.

Then I heard him running away.

I looked over my shoulder, his path swung wide to a third man, a tall skinny, Caucasian punk with straggly, weakly bleached dreads and a long gaunt face—his gun was trying to keep up with me.

Mr. Ages' teeth clamped on the arm with the gun.

The man kicked him.

He let out a yelp—I'd never heard him make any sound of pain before.

I was nearly to them.

Mr. Ages fell on his side from the blow.
He was getting up ~~when he was shot~~—then he just dropped.

I started screaming.

The man leveled the gun at me. I saw the blood pouring from his lower arm. I could see the fleshy mechanics of his arm through the rushing blood. He looked dumbly at the wound. Then he ran.

I chased for only seconds—Mr. Ages was more important.

Busy bodies were already there.

I thought I'd found Heaven.

I don't know if I was too right or more wrong than I have ever been.

If all goes well, I'll be back to take care of Mr. Ages. If not, he will be wrapped in the shower curtain, in the tub. I have left a note with him.

If he's not there and you've found this, then I'm not back yet or I've been hurt and won't be back.

If they've mortally wounded me, I won't die before I've taken care of him. Not if I'm that close. I won't.

I'm ready.
I'm ready.
I'm ready.

I am ready.

I've got *Ether* by Nothingface in my head. And that is good—
I'm *really* fucking feeling it.
Like the victims of NIMH. We're not rats, not anymore.

At least, I'm not.

I don't feel strong. After all of this—I don't know if there ever
was such a thing as strong or brave. But there has always been
hurt. There has always been anger. There has always been
terror.

This needs to happen. When anything matters this much—fear
can't be an issue... or an excuse.

I don't really expect to survive.

So I'm leaving my things here so they don't get ruined.

If you have any compassion or honesty left in you, please give
me until morning to return before you ransack or destroy all
that is left of me. After that, not that I could do anything about
it, but *I* want you to know that you are welcome to whatever
you think will help you—I recommend the book in my pack.
It's missing its cover.

If you found this, I am probably dead, but please wait or try
and find me. If I'm alive, I don't want to be alone.
If I am dead, please kill me again.

Sincerely,
Tamberlin Miner

Enjoy the fruit cocktail. It lasts about 2 years. You will like the Slim Fast. I feel that time is running out—even as I watch the seconds steadfastly add up on my watch. Maybe you can use the time. I don't want it anymore.

I've lived 253 days. That feels pretty significant.

I'm lucky.

You are too.

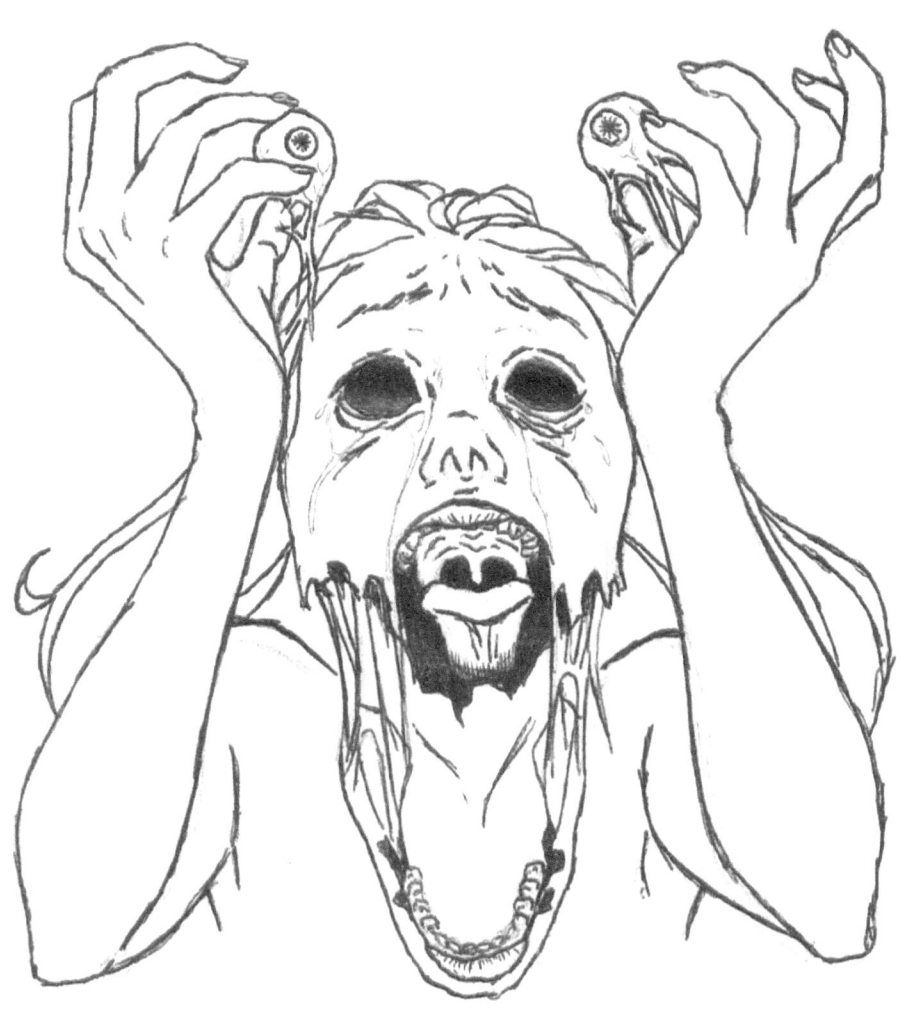

...Sanctuary

DEAD   TOWN

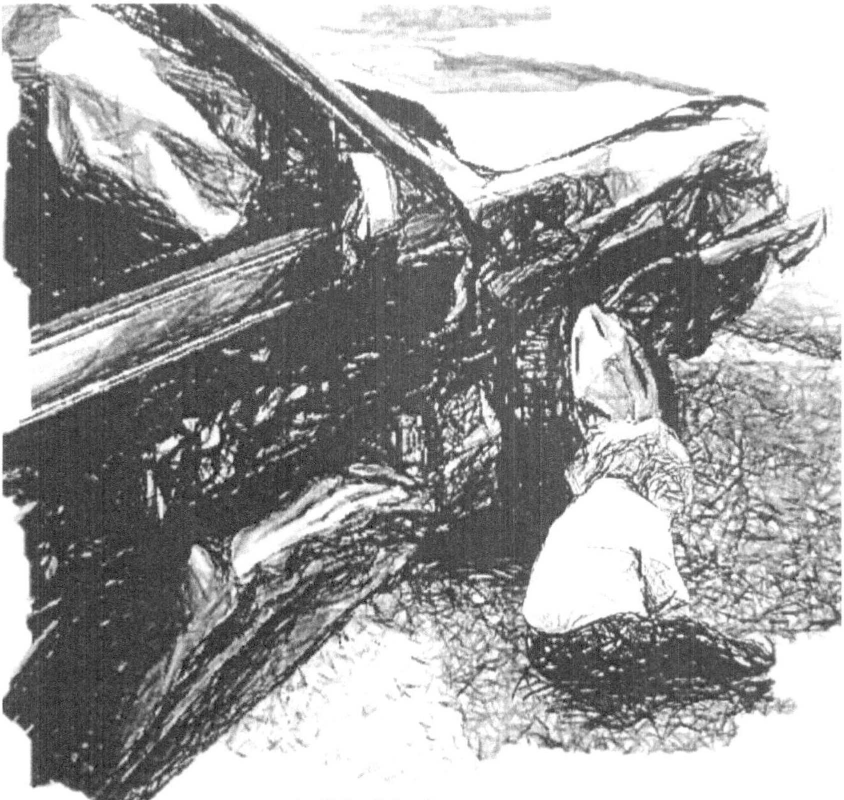

...left behind

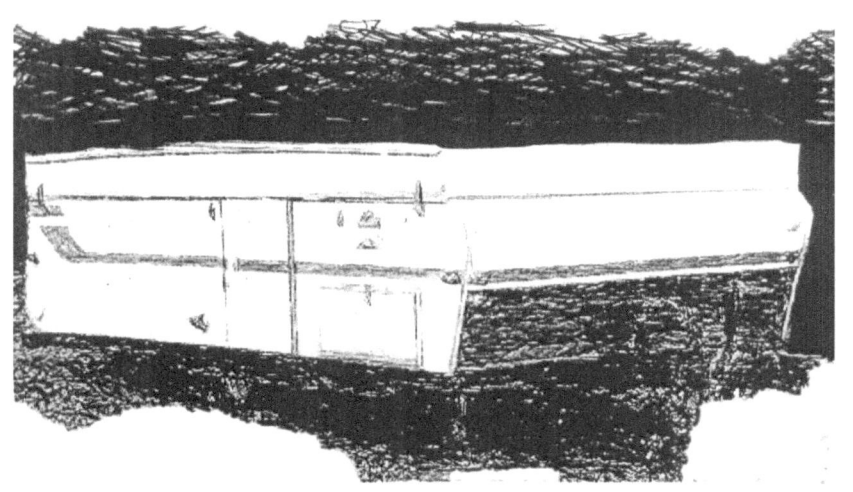

Seigecraft

ZOMBIE TRACKING CHART

Name	Description	DOD 2.0
Lazarus	The first undead: missing half his face	July 5
Red	Red shirt	Sept 7
Farmer	older guy with bibs	
Murphy	"Murphy Brown" blonde, executive type	Aug 3
Waldo	Striped shirt and glasses	
Turtle	Broken collar and shoulders on long neck and HUGE body	Oct 19
Mary Anne	brunette w/pigtails	July 29
Postman	Mailman	
Bingo	seems to pop up randomly	
Harry	Hairy	
Narcissus	seems to notice the water, probably just frogs	Aug 3
Adam	naked man whose crotch has been eaten away	
Barney	short, thick blonde w/no legs	Oct 2
John Doe	white t-shirt, jeans, really "normal"	
Bull	huge, beefy younger man – atypical linebacker type	
Jeremy	middle-aged man with snow white hair	
Dolly	heavy woman, large ratty hair, huge cha-chas, walks hunched over	Aug 2
Cathy	regular young woman	Aug 5
Brat Pack	assorted school children – always in pack (x8)	
		-1 July 8
		-1 July 22
		-3 Aug17
Monty	looks like a Python; I don't remember which.	July 24
Hans the Nord	male with long white-blonde hair	Sep 15
Quazi	The shirtless man with a clearly broken back	
Wilt	The zombie who's at least 6'8 or 9	
Frankenstein	Description cannot do justice: To see him is to know he is.	

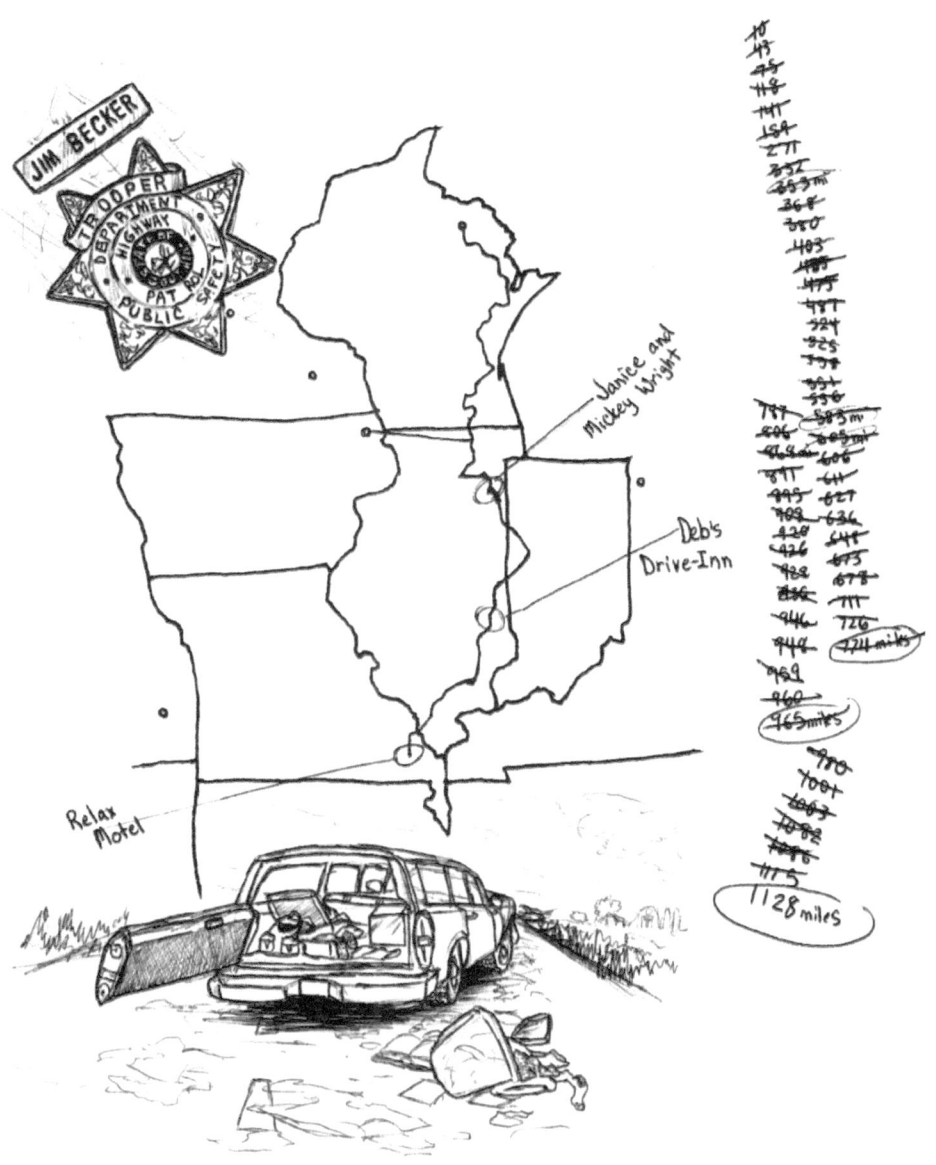

"Who are you…?"

COPYRIGHT

DEDICATION

This book is dedicated to friends:

To childhood friends, wondering what became of you.

To childhood friends that stuck around to be adult friends.
To new friends, especially Sandy, one of the most considerate people I've ever known.
To my sister, who I'm grateful is also my friend.
Each of you is a blessing who has improved my life and stabilized my existence. It has been so much fun corrupting each other!
Thank you for everything.

To animal friends, both past and present, who, in their unfailing love, perfect honesty, and innocence, are constant reminders of what should really matter in our lives.

You keep me going—because being a human can be hard.

Oh, and this is also dedicated to my high school Spanish class, because I promised my first book would be.

ABOUT the AUTHOR

I have a Bachelor of Arts Degree in Writing from Bemidji State University in Minnesota. I am a freelance artist, making ends meet by working at a nearby hospital.

I got into writing and art as an escapist—I've always been a daydreamer. I believe there is no better way to find a story to tell than giving your imagination a free hand. I hope I'll get to share everything I've conjured when willing myself, my soul, my consciousness—whichever—into a world or a life more interesting than my own.

Tamberlin's Account is my first novel. Other works include *Dark Dreams and the Wizardry of Blank Stares*, a collection of early poetry.

Thanks for reading about me.

www.ingramcontent.com/pod-product-compliance
Lightning Source LLC
Chambersburg PA
CBHW022145170626
46807CB00005B/2087